T0128934

Zoe Senesh

King Solomon's Troubles

KING SOLOMON'S TROUBLES

Holman Christian Standard Bible (HCSB)
Copyright © 1999, 2000, 2002, 2003, 2009 by Holman Bible Publishers, Nashville Tennessee. All rights reserved.

iUniverse books may be ordered through booksellers or by contacting:

iUniverse
1663 Liberty Drive
Bloomington, IN 47403
www.iuniverse.com
1-800-Authors (1-800-288-4677)

ISBN: 978-1-4759-8638-9 (sc)
ISBN: 978-1-4759-8636-5 (hc)
ISBN: 978-1-4759-8637-2 (e)

Library of Congress Control Number: 2013907030

Print information available on the last page.

iUniverse rev. date: 04/27/2017

But mankind is born for trouble as surely as sparks fly upward.

Job 5:7
Holman Christian Standard Bible (2009)

chapter 1

I COULD HAVE SEX with you, Rachel mused, slightly embarrassed at her thoughts, as she looked at the man she had known for several years. *But of course I won't.* Her blue eyes sparkled. After he smiled awkwardly at her from twenty feet away, she waited for him to walk over and talk to her. But he marched down the aisle of the grocery store with his eyes and shoulders forward in a serious, driven manner, as if food shopping was an important business decision. *Guess he doesn't want sex with me.* She laughed off the momentary fantasy of eloping with him in a wild whirlwind of passion. For a few glorious seconds, she'd imagined seducing him, enjoying him, pleasuring him.

She impulsively turned and ran after him, stuttering out, "Hey, can I ask you something?" He turned abruptly, astounded at her sudden lunge in his direction. "What do you think about the latest article about the psychological consequences of international aid in the *International Perspectives in Psychology* journal?" He stood still, looking a little stunned, and then awkwardly said, "I haven't read it yet, but I will." He looked down at her breasts, outlined by her sundress, and his eyes widened. Then he turned around and bolted, scurrying away from her like a lizard disappearing into the shadows of the day.

Some men are bizarre creatures, Rachel thought. *They devour you with their eyes, and then when you try to talk with them, they run away.* Her bracelets made a pleasant, metallic clinking sound as she continued down the aisle, focusing on her food shopping. She selected fresh romaine lettuce, warm rosy tomatoes, long organic carrots, and firm, ripe cucumbers. *How Freudian of me,* she thought, smiling. She paid for her food and then walked out into the muggy heat of the New York summer.

Rachel sat down at a nearby café table and ordered an iced cappuccino. She stretched out her long, clean-shaven legs under the table and adjusted the strap of her yellow sundress. Pulling her thick, curly, brown hair up off her neck, she used a napkin to soak up the perspiration on her forehead and neck. She thought about when she'd met the man in the store at work five years ago. He was the president of the non-profit agency where she worked while she finished her master's degree in psychology. He was an introvert and often acted befuddled and awkward around her. But he talked fast and excitedly to her whenever the topic was work-related. Sometimes he gave her a big smile. At other times, he would appear to be overcome with guilt or fear during a conversation, and then he would withdraw deep into himself in front of Rachel's eyes. She had never seen anyone withdraw deep into his thoughts. It was like a switch had turned off—from apparently engaged in conversation, he would retreat into the recesses of his mind. He'd also had the annoying habit of abruptly cutting off a conversation and running off to who-knew-what task or destination. As a budding sex therapist, Rachel suspected his paradoxical behavior was either due to anxiety or strong levels of sexual tension. *These are often are one and the same,* she thought as she wistfully remembered how they used to interact.

Rachel started calling him Mr. Hit-and-Run to her friends. She learned how to gauge his moment of departure by watching his shifting eyes and antsy feet. The most obvious clue to his imminent departure was the inability to look Rachel in the eye. When he was ready to bolt, his hazel eyes would dance around, flitting here and there, and would not meet her eyes directly. At first she thought it was shyness that made him want to run, but that did not make sense, because he was bold in so many ways. He could be very articulate in front of audiences, a precise and thorough speaker, a compassionate humanist who often came up with new ideas for how to help people in third-world countries, and a courageous advocate who could cite five examples for every statement that he made. In other words, he was a brilliant man.

Rachel and Mr. Hit-and-Run found business reasons for sharing a coffee or lunch together. They laughed and chatted energetically about all sorts of work-related issues. He did not talk about personal issues, but she saw his sexual desire ignite when his eyes lingered over her breasts and then fixated on her mouth as she was drinking through a straw on a hot summer day. Then he began slipping double entendres into the conversation. Rachel started to think that he wanted to date her, or at least wanted her. She was aware that she had a curvaceous body, full breasts, sensual lips, a warm smile, and a cheerful grin encircled by dimples. She knew that she was subtly attractive in a natural way. One day at lunch, she asked him if he'd like to go to dinner and to a show with her. He tersely replied, "Why do you ask that? That cannot and should not be." And then he'd run away, like a horse that shied from a rustling in the grass, thinking it was a snake.

Rachel watched New Yorkers and tourists walk by the café as she sipped her cold drink, tilting her face toward the summer sun. Suddenly, her eyebrows flicked upward and her eyes widened. She quickly dug through her purse and retrieved a pen and a small spiral-bound notebook. Her eyes fixed on the paper, and she scribbled quickly.

> Come to me,
> My love,
> And I will
> Give you
> My sweetness.

And we will spin
A gentle web
Of happiness
In this chaotic world
That crushes the soul
Who shows weakness.
Come to me,
My lover,
And I will
Fall to my knees,
And we will
Experience
What gives you
Delirious joy
And what
Makes me
Speechless.

chapter 2

GOD THUNDERED TO SOLOMON in his dreams, "Get up—you are in My presence."

Solomon awoke with a yelp and sat up in bed, staring with glazed eyes out into the hazy night. His voluptuous lover was cloaked by a veil of her own long black hair. She mumbled incoherently and turned her head away, too tired from the couple's energetic entwining to awake at loud noises. Solomon shook his head and whispered to her, "Just a dream." Then he slipped back under the layers of warmth and slid over to encircle his nighttime companion.

But God did not let him off easy and returned to Solomon after he went back to sleep. He heard the voice of God again in his dreams. God called his name and said, "Get up. I have work for you."

Solomon yelled out, "What? Who are you?" and then sat up again. He jumped to the floor and strolled around his chambers, which were richly hung with embroidered linen. He did not see anyone who could have said such a thing to him. After signaling to his guards at the door to stand down, he walked outside into the courtyard and sat for some time near a soothingly trickling fountain. He listened to the night birds singing to each other and felt a fragrant night breeze moving warmly across the desert floor into his palace. God did not reply. After waiting about an hour in anticipation but hearing no more words, Solomon slipped back into his bed and drifted asleep, cradled in human heat and darkness.

For a third time, God called to him. This time, Solomon was ready to listen. "Yes, God, I am here."

God said, "I want you to build a temple so glorious that others who are worshipping their gods made of dirt and clay will know that I am who I am."

Solomon, in awe of this request, whispered into the darkness, "Yes, I will do this, my Lord." He fell to his knees and bowed his head. A sense of peace came over him, and he knew that he would somehow find a way to build this temple.

But sleep did not come again to Solomon that night. He paced his chambers again, thinking, *Why me?* He thought of his father, King David, who had fought and won many battles in his life. Solomon had never fought wars with his neighbors. He did not understand why God, if indeed it was God, wanted him to build a temple, because he had not proven himself to be worthy in any way for that monumental task. His father did tell him once that God would not allow him to build a temple because he had too much blood on his hands, although he was victorious in many wars and had protected Israel.

Maybe that voice was me imagining things? Solomon pondered. Solomon sat down and carefully wrote out his thoughts:

Who am I, God,
To speak with you?
Who am I, God,
To receive from you?
Who am I, God,
To stand before you?

I, Solomon, am a man
Of many troubles
Of many foibles
And do not deserve
Such riches and fame
When my mind is full of
great longing and shame.

chapter 3

THE WHITE AND BLUE Israeli flag draped softly from the railing of the two-story Bauhaus-style apartment overlooking Dizengoff Street. Sarah peered over the railing to scan the chaotic black hole of ambulances, bodies laying on the street, high-pitched voices yelling into cell phones, and shocked, frantic people wailing in despair. The anguished cries bothered her more than the bloody scene—the animal-like, uncontrollable, inconsolable wailing tapped something deep in her and frightened her. She felt nausea in the pit of her stomach and ran to her closet-sized bathroom, where she remained for over an hour.

Sitting crookedly in the tiled shower with her legs propped up against the wall, Sarah leaned her forehead on the cool tiles to try to calm her pulsing headache. She rolled her head sideways to place her cheek against the smooth tiles. She struggled not to be sick to her stomach and tightly wrapped her arms around her midsection. There she sat, cushioned from the chaos of the street and sheltered in the embrace of the secure space of her small bathroom—the very space she had cursed when she felt tired of her life in Israel and wanted to escape to freer pastures. The sirens continued. In the kitchen, the Voice of Israel radio station kept reporting news of the event and the rising death toll. She was too confused, nauseated, and fatigued to get up and turn off the radio.

When the warm glow of the sunset spread across her living room wall and reflected under the bathroom door, Sarah finally dragged herself out of the bathroom and picked up her cell phone to call Moshe, her current boyfriend of eight months.

"Where were you?" he shouted. "I left twelve messages on your phone. You made me sick with worry!" he spouted in an Israeli accent that Sarah always savored.

"Moshe, I was hiding in my bathroom. You know how scared I get after a suicide bomb. This one was so close … so close I could see the bodies and the bus. If I had gone to buy bread I might be dead right now!" she screamed at him.

Sarah started crying, tears flowing, stumbling over her words, and Moshe began consoling her.

Moshe said, "Stay where you are. I am coming."

Typically, Sarah would have turned his statement into a sexual joke, but at this moment, she felt no sexual desire. She had heard of stories of couples mating furiously after a close call with a suicide bomb. She imagined that fear of the ending of their lives injected an almost uncontrollable energy to experience, to savor touch, to feel skin, to cling to another body, as if to conquer an inevitable death. It was the ultimate fight-or-flight response. But at this moment, performing a sexual act was incomprehensible to her.

Sarah walked over to her large window overlooking the street and saw a water truck with a man spraying the street with pressurized water. She knew the procedure from TV news—for hours after the bombing, forensic experts in white hazard suits wearing special boots would comb the ground for evidence about the type of bomb that was used. They carefully collected human remains and analyzed them in the lab to determine victims' identities. After the forensic experts in their strange white suits were finished, then the clean-up crew moved in to remove all traces of the bombing. Often, plate-glass shop windows had to be replaced and cars had to be towed from the scene. Because of the quick clean-up, by the next day any pedestrian who did not know the location of the bomb would be unable to discover where it had detonated. It was one way Israelis coped with repeated bombings, erasing and rebuilding as quickly as possible to return society to apparently normal functioning. This was their *sabra*, or cactus-like spirit—the prickly, tough exterior covering a sweet interior—that had helped them survive the decades of fighting numerous wars with the British who occupied the *Eretz Yisrael*, the land of Israel, and with their Arab neighbors.

Sarah felt irritated and vicious as she watched the street cleaners. She yelled out in her empty, quiet apartment, "Why this madness? What the hell are they doing? Where are my damn cigarettes?" The sounds echoed off her tiled floor, sparse furniture, and walls adorned with a few pictures. Her hands jittered, and she frenetically scrambled to find a cigarette. At last she lit one. She sat on her couch, staring numbly at the fashion channel on the TV. She turned up the volume to drown out the street noise. The European techno music thumped loudly as the undernourished, pale models strutted down the runway.

Moshe arrived, looking distracted and disheveled, even with his buzz-cut hair and shaven face. He walked in and stopped at the kitchen table. Sarah could see that he was puzzled at her lack of greeting. Usually, she ran to him and hugged and kissed him energetically. But she said nothing to him when he unlocked her apartment door and walked to the table. He got some water from the refrigerator and leaned on the edge of Sarah's kitchen counter. "Well?" he said.

"What the hell took you so long?" Sarah screamed. "What's wrong with you? Don't you care about me?" she barked.

He tried to defend himself, but Sarah continued on her offensive path. "You're never around when I need you!" she screamed.

"I was at work ... I called you twelve times!"

"That's no excuse. There was a bombing. Right here! Right

outside my window!" Sarah ran to her couch and dove beneath her Indian-décor throw pillows.

Moshe knew enough about Sarah and about women to know what she needed. He followed her to the couch and sat down beside her to comfort her. He encircled her with his army-hardened, sun-tanned arms, holding her tightly while she cried.

chapter 4

RACHEL SUNK INTO HER overstuffed black leather couch, scanned her living room, and threw her feet up on a round footstool. She closed her eyes and pictured the range of clients she had seen that week in her therapy practice. *The human race can be categorized into four groups: people who derive their ego satisfaction from sex, money, power, or family,* Rachel thought. *Yes, indeed.*

Rachel's view was that attention, work, control, and babies were the gravitational fields of the ego. Some people feasted with great bravado from all four categories. And some changed their ego source over the years, first deriving major ego gratification from sex and then, within a few decades, identifying themselves with money and its first cousin, power. Topping off the cappuccino of sex with a sweet dollop of family, they slurped it down in the triumphant venture of their lives on this planet.

But some people claim that they do not need any ego gratification, Rachel thought. She smiled wryly as she remembered all the quirky clients she had seen as a sex therapist in the past few years. The ones who claimed that they didn't have ego needs were often the very same people who experienced extreme success and pleasure in all four categories. *Guess it's easier to say that you don't need something when it is right under your nose and when you are so satiated by abundance that you become sick of it.*

She grabbed the book she was reading on ancient Israel. *King*

Solomon, of Biblical fame, was like that. He had sex, money, power, and family, plus lots and lots of women. But he also claimed that it was all worthless in the end. She paused. *Or maybe he realized that he was not defined by his possessions and women? Not like he had any needs that weren't fulfilled—he was king over the small territory called Israel, even though it was a dusty land full of scrubby bushes inhabited by emaciated donkeys and tired farmers. Ah, but the women ... all historical accounts indicate that he wedded and bedded, or just bedded, an enormous number of women. The Bible said he had seven hundred wives and three hundred concubines!*

Rachel snorted. *There are a lot of men nowadays who'd love to have what King Solomon had—riches, power, and women.* She thought about some of her male clients who had access and power. *They enjoy themselves for several decades and then they run to therapy when they lose their money and power for whatever reason. These burned-out, middle-age men come into my office and complain that life is meaningless! I do not like such clients.*

She was careful about what she wrote in her therapy notes, because the court system could request the notes if any legal problems involved her clients. She would write that such men "lacked self-awareness and insight," but she thought they were stupid and greedy. For years, those men had lived a life of partying, sex, and drugs, buying whatever expensive items they had a taste for. Then they came into her office complaining about their meaningless lives and how they couldn't trust anyone. *Just ship them off to the slums of India or the refugee camps of Africa for a month and they'd be cured,* she thought. *They have forgotten about empathy, compassion, and giving. They can't fathom any joy that is not connected with sex or drugs.*

She thought more about King Solomon's life. *Like so many of the clients that I see in my sex therapy sessions, his life was full of contradictions. He was a man of excess, yet a man of discipline. He was a man of rules, yet a man of erotic abandon. He had great creativity, yet was known as a man of reason and justice. That was his paradox—a dialectic of pleasure and logic. He liked women, but at the same time he was one of the most intellectual men of his kingdom. He wrote beautifully. Many books of the Bible or Torah are believed to be his writings—Proverbs, Ecclesiastes, and Song of Songs.*

Rachel remembered some of the Biblical stories that she'd read growing up as a Christian. Solomon's father was the renowned King David. *David was another man full of contradictions. He was a restless soul, tormented by rage and depression, yet capable of great emotion and poetry. King David was a man who made his own rules. He stole another man's wife and arranged her husband's death. The stolen woman was Bathsheba, King Solomon's mother. Yet King David was famous for fighting in the name of his God and for his nation. King David often sang praises to God but was also quick to pull out his sword. Both Solomon and David were pleasure-seekers, men of the flesh and men of power, but also men of God. And that is the ultimate paradox.*

chapter 5

SOME NIGHTS, KING SOLOMON got up after his lover fell asleep and settled on the porch overlooking the city. There he quietly watched the stars, the night watchmen, and the occasional man straddling a donkey that was clicking across the deserted town square. Sometimes at night, a blanket of peace settled over Jerusalem, like the serene sensation that permeated the air every Friday when the Sabbath started at dusk. This was one of those nights—the tranquility was palpable.

Yet Solomon was not at peace. Lately, fear stalked him, stabbing at his heart and gnawing at his nocturnal thoughts. While all around him was quiet and serene, he sat in silence, battling with the invisible forces that tried to conquer him. He felt enraged without knowing why. He tried to understand the jumbled, inarticulate thoughts and black anger that seem to slide into him like waves. He stubbornly refused to submit, to let those forces win. He knew that if he stopped fighting, he would slip deeper into the hole he was feeling.

His father, King David, had battled with sadness and forlornness for many years. King David had told his son that the only time he felt alive was on the battlefield. And his father had said to him once, "I know what I am fighting for in war, but when I am at home, Bathsheba and I battle over things for no reason."

When Solomon was growing up, he often watched his father run out the door to escape Bathsheba's wrath. His mother was bitter about many things. After her first husband had been killed because King David intentionally sent him to the front of the battle lines, she married King David and became his queen. But then she lost her first son, David's child. After her child died, it was as if she turned a corner. She became enraged with David over little things—the many household things that he could not control. In response to her bitter words, King David would go for a walk out in the desert evening, soothed by a cool breeze and the dull light of the moon. But Bathsheba thought he left to visit another woman, which made her even more furious and cold to him when he returned.

Back in his chambers, King David avoided Bathsheba. He found a quiet room and stroked his harp, composing songs. His thoughts were often bitter, black with anger and full of melancholy. The only way he felt that he could get through the day was calming himself through music. He wrote down his words, seeking guidance from God, whom he knew was there. He kept asking his God for a cure for his painful loneliness.

As a young man grappling with the fierce arrival of his own sexuality, Solomon puzzled over his parents' strange relations. They fluctuated between friction and arguments and passionate glances and pleading apologies. Solomon suspected that King David rejoiced when he heard that another war was brewing on Israel's battlefield. King David seemed energized and almost ecstatic when a new conflict was beginning. Solomon thought that war gave his father a reason to escape harsh Bathsheba and feel powerful once again. Solomon never wanted to live as his father did; he saw a man who was unhappy whenever he was around Bathsheba, despite his great authority over others.

Solomon loved the company of women. But he knew that he could not tolerate them for very long. He liked to extract their sweetness, like a hummingbird sucking in nectar, and then run off to tend to his more manly duties, like building things, holding court, arguing religious points, and racing on donkeys and camels against other men for sport.

When Solomon became king, his days were filled with discussions, persuasions, debates, and lively meals filled with stories of battlefield heroes and conquerors of nations. He reserved his nights for women. Women rarely spoke at his evening meals, but they served him food, cleared his dishes, poured his wine, fetched his cloak, and rubbed his feet. He hungrily eyed the women at his banquets while he talked with the men and laughed at anecdotes told by his advisors. His advisors knew enough about Solomon to invite to the nightly banquet only women who were willing and able to be with Solomon if he beckoned them. So his advisors never invited married women to the banquet, except Solomon's wives.

Solomon wandered around his bedchamber. He felt mentally exhausted, yet physically he was agitated. He was torn between two opposing forces, unable to think yet unable to sleep. He stumbled around, trying to focus, and then he tried to sleep. Neither approach worked. So he lay on his bed, numb, eyes wide open and shiny, unable to think about anything.

When golden rays brightened the horizon and the city came to life with sound and movement, he rushed out into the market square, his sleepy guards running after him. He ran down the alleys that were slowly filling with people getting water, feeding their donkeys and camels, and loading their carts for a day of marketplace haggling.

Solomon drank in the movement, the sounds of children waking up, and the color of sky and desert. Suddenly, he felt great pain in his right eye. He stumbled and then stopped, feeling around his watering eye, trying to locate the source of the pain. He could not open his eyes. He heard a woman's voice say, "Let me see." She approached him, leaning in so close that he could smell her musky sweet odor. Her hands gently opened his eye and deftly removed something. The pain ceased. "It was a piece of straw," she said gently. He opened up his still-watering eye to see a pair of soft, brown eyes framed in a rough cotton veil. She smiled at him and said, "You will be fine," touching his hand lightly. For once in his life, he stood silently, unable to say one word in response. She laughed with a musical sound and then turned away from him.

Solomon's guards rushed in to see what their king needed. It took only seconds for Solomon to communicate the story. He pushed through his ring of security men and looked around the marketplace. He did not see his comforter. He frantically asked each merchant, "Who was that woman?" Most shrugged or shook their heads. He ran around the courtyards and alleys looking for her until his guards were panting. Solomon stopped for some water and waited for his guards to catch up with him. He grimaced. "Where did she go? Why did she leave?" He tiredly stood and gestured to his guards that they should return home with him.

Upon returning to his bedchambers, Solomon found he was no longer in the grip of the unseen forces, and he finally felt sleepy. He returned to his bed, entwined himself with his sleep-drunk partner, and performed a bed dance with her. *Maybe I should keep this one around?* he thought. He fell asleep quickly with the noise from the street blanketing him and the warm arms of his lover encircling him.

Despite little sleep after his restless night and early morning wanderings around the marketplace, King Solomon arose, feeling rejuvenated. He once again refreshed himself with the lovely lady who willingly had joined him in his previous night's journey. *Maybe I should marry her?* he thought. He quickly left the royal chambers, grabbing a handful of flat bread and dates, eating them with a slight smile. He ran down the dusty street to the meeting place, where the architects were arguing over the angling of small corners, directions and heights of windows, and colors of the future temple.

Solomon's mind was lively, sparkling with energy gained from the combination of food, running down the street, elation over constructing the temple, and the cinnamon warmth of a woman. He asked the workers questions, mediated disagreements, and extracted a decision relevant to the upcoming work on the temple's walls.

If only humans were as easy to understand as the process of building a temple, King Solomon mulled as he watched a group of young, beautifully alive adolescent girls talk, modestly holding their veils to keep them from falling from their heads. Solomon did not see the knowing looks his advisors and managers exchanged. He knew he wanted to marry again. His most recent wife, Lilith, had rejected his embraces and no longer visited him in his bedchamber. Lilith lived in her own separate quarters, sharing them with a maid. The sweet milk of their marital bed had long ago curdled, and what remained was not tasty.

Yet he and Lilith could still speak cordially when she brought the children to visit their king-father. The children, whose ages ranged between three and nine, were aware enough to tremble in the presence of their father, with his booming voice, gold-plated chest armor, flowing robes, and flashing eyes. Only the youngest of her children overcame the power of this commanding presence. During every visit, Lilith's little girl would waddle up to the throne with a flower, rock, or piece of bread in her hand and would fling her cargo at King Solomon. Then she turned and ran, shrieking with laughter. This never failed to make him laugh. He would swing down to pick the child up and then lift her above his head. She squealed with delight. Everyone in the courtyard chuckled at the sight.

King Solomon once said to this child, "You are a joy to me, and you will be a blessing to everyone you meet." Ayala was the name Solomon gave to her at the moment of her painful birth, when Lilith was finally released from thirty-two hours of labor and lay exhausted on the bed. At that exact moment, Solomon began to adore Ayala's soft, dark eyes. In the first moments of her life, those eyes opened and stared directly at him, innocent and full of wonder. Since that moment, there was never fear in Ayala's eyes, only warmth, when she saw King Solomon. And she made him laugh like no other child. She instinctively ran toward him at every meeting, no matter who was holding her hand. King Solomon felt the pride of fatherhood but also amazement at Ayala's trust and absolute joy. *If only a woman could be that way toward me*, he thought.

chapter 6

As an American living in Tel Aviv, Sarah enjoyed status as a foreigner, exotic to certain Israeli men, including her current boyfriend, Moshe. A gentle, slender woman with long blond hair, blue eyes, and high cheekbones, Sarah's appearance also attracted scores of Israeli men who were tired of home-grown, vivacious, assertive Israeli women. These were not the agitated men who lingered at the Tel Aviv malls, pretending to look at the books and jewelry in the center stalls between stores while their eyes darted around and followed every footstep connected to clicking high heels.

The agenda of the mall-scoping men was to get sex as quickly and as painlessly as possible, preferably for free. These men looked for the young Israeli girls who were ready to gain experience in the sexual department. But the men attracted to Sarah had different agendas. Many desired an exotic breed of foreign women, especially American. Being able to say to their male friends that they had an American girlfriend gave them huge bragging rights. Not only had they overcome a woman's sexual barrier, but that of a coveted American woman.

Some men who were fans of Sarah pursued foreign women because they wanted to avoid the mandatory three-year military service in the Israel Defense Force (IDF), which was followed by mandatory service in the IDF reserves for the next three decades. Marrying was an acceptable way to avoid being called a military coward. These men sought a socially acceptable reason to leave the pressure cooker called Israel but would never admit their true reasons for pursuing and marrying foreign women. They could just marry and emigrate. They would not have to participate in public demonstrations against the power of the IDF and its policies or join peace-activist groups. These men dreamed of an easy escape. They would gleefully cite the urban legend, often discussed in male locker rooms and soldiers' barracks, that American women were the best women in the world for pleasing their men in bed. And that was a good enough reason to chase after American girls and then to hightail it out of Israel.

To many Israeli men, it made no difference that Sarah was technically not Jewish because her mother was not Jewish. For centuries, the laws of Judaism had defined Jewish heritage as being carried only by the mother. Thus, if a mother was not Jewish but the father was, then their son or daughter technically could not claim to be Jewish according to the Orthodox rabbis, even if they went through a bar or bat mitzvah at age thirteen.

Sarah's mother had been born and bred as a Catholic in the emerald green fields outside of Belfast until her parents immigrated to America. Sarah's father was a European Jew who immigrated to America from the Czech Republic, which explained his penchant for baroque classical music and crystal goblets at dinnertime. This also explained Sarah's innate fondness for sparkly jewelry, both real and synthetic. She was raised in the suburbia of Connecticut, with its groomed lawns, three-car garages, and private schools. Her parents decided to make a radical change and move to Israel when she was fourteen.

When Sarah became an adolescent, she developed a strong dislike of the zeitgeist of her Connecticut neighborhood. Everyone greeted each other cordially at the mailboxes or when walking their dogs. All her neighbors proudly went to either church or synagogue every week. But during the various holidays, they plastered their houses and yards with Christmas decorations and lights or Hanukkah symbols and lights. Sarah grew to hate what she viewed as a flaunting of spirituality. She thought that it was more like decorating for their faith than about religious practice, a type of spiritual materialism—garishly exhibiting their religious affiliation like a membership card to an exclusive club that offered the ultimate prize of a guaranteed place in heaven.

Most Israeli men who pursued Sarah did not obsess over the specific details of her Jewish heritage or her religious beliefs, but rather, the flow of her long blond hair and the click of the high heels that carried her shapely legs.

Orthodox Jewish men, sporting black-and-white outfits that reflected their close adherence to nineteenth-century Jewish religious tradition, would pursue Sarah and ask a few standard screening questions, such as, "Are you Jewish? Is your mother a Jew?" Even though Sarah did not want their interest, it felt good to be desired. She quickly learned how to shut them down by simply replying, "My mother is a Christian." The Orthodox men would look at her with horror and immediately turn their backs to her. *Sick bastards*, she thought every time it happened. "As if I would ever want you!" she started saying under her breath to their backs as they scurried away.

Upon arriving in Israel, Sarah realized that these black-and-white Orthodox men were not only black and white in dress code but also in their thinking. They would never consider Sarah as a potential marriage partner, given that her mother was not Jewish. Sarah also learned that she could never have a legal wedding ceremony in Israel, because the Orthodox had tight control over the country's rules pertaining to marriage. The Orthodox still did not allow civil marriages in Israel, only religious marriages performed by a rabbi.

Every time an Orthodox man "screened" her with questions about her heritage and her religious beliefs, Sarah got angry. She recalled the latest attempt by an Orthodox man to seduce or marry her. *It is rather interesting that Orthodox Jews assume that being a Jew is an elevated status of humanity, that being a Jew means you are part of a more spiritually pure race*, she thought as she wandered into her favorite air-conditioned mall. *One day they will realize that following religious rules does not necessarily make you a kind, decent person!* She sniffed a perfume bottle on the display counter.

And I know my Bible stories enough to know the Jewish nation often used to stray from God. But of course, God always welcomed them back. She paused to look at the new display of her favorite brand of make-up. *Many strayed, but the decent ones tried to go back and follow God's rules. So maybe the Orthodox Jews have something there—following God's rules is extremely important. But the main problem I see with the rule-obsessed Orthodox view is that you can be a rule-abider and still be a nasty person. And who knows why they even follow the rules? Maybe they are deathly afraid of not following the rules? Obedience out of fear? How is that spiritually advanced?* she thought.

It does not matter much, because I would never marry an Orthodox man, and he would never marry me, Sarah thought as she veered toward the counter with sparkly costume jewelry. She leaned on the counter, peering in to get a closer look at the necklaces. Sarah heard a soft whistle behind her and glanced up. Three young Israeli men in military uniforms were smiling at her and slowly walking by. Each had his eyes fixated on a different part of her body: black high heels, tight skirt, revealing shirt. *Yeah, I am quite a marketplace, boys!* she thought gleefully.

She knew that the non-religious Israeli men were attracted to her because of American-brand stereotypes: cute, blond, seemingly submissive cheerleaders. These guys did not care whether Sarah's mother was Jewish or not, though they knew that their own mothers would ask that question if they brought Sarah home to share their Sabbath meal. The issue of her heritage did not register in their minds as potently as her long, golden hair and her four-inch heels did.

chapter 7

As RACHEL SAT IN the airplane one-quarter full of adolescents going to Israel for a summer program, she mused, *Many people think that people who are religious are not sexual. They are so very, very wrong.* She thought about the hundreds of clients she had counseled during sex and couples therapy. *I think it is often the opposite. After the first few months of an endorphin-high triggered by being with a new partner, I think secular people are less able to sustain sexual interactions with one partner than religious people. The secular ones often get restless and seek different sexual stimuli in the form of a new lover. I think religious people often respond more freely, openly, and honestly with their partner, because they may actually like the person that they are with.*

From what I can tell, religious people have more secure relationships, and they know where the boundaries are in their partnership. That means they can really trust their partner. So they respond with more fervor than people who have sneaky sex with strangers. Sure, sneaky sex gives some people an adrenaline rush, but they typically don't share the deeper parts of themselves with strangers. Even prostitutes are guarded about sharing their real selves with their clients. This is why most prostitutes fake orgasms and never have real orgasms. Former prostitutes tell me that if they ever had a real orgasm with a client, they knew it was the time to stop inviting the client back. They knew they had crossed a line. Rachel chuckled to herself. She knew that even prostitutes had lines and boundaries, which was not what most people believed about sex workers.

Rachel kept thinking about the faces of the many men and women who had come to her for sex therapy and who had revealed some of their more painful secrets. She saw many people who were sex addicts or who had just broken up with their partner. But sometimes couples would come to her, asking her to help them become a better couple. That was the most satisfying kind of therapy, because she helped people either find love again or find peace if they needed to separate.

Rachel observed the woman sitting to her left. She wore clothes typical of an Orthodox Jewish woman. Rachel thought, *Sometimes it takes a little while for religious people to get used to the sexual encounter and to feel freer in sexual expression with their partner, because they have had to repress their sexual behaviors for many years, due to religious rules. But their sexual forces are layered with emotional and psychological energy that once triggered, give intensity to the sexual encounter that makes it even more potent. And these clients are the ones most grateful for my therapy.* She chuckled to herself. *People would never guess this.*

She had many former clients in the religious communities around New York. They knew her ideas about sexuality and religion, so her schedule was always full. *I think it is good to teach moral rules to kids, especially about sex, and then hope that those rules are integrated as they grow up. I think that they will be happier in the long term, even if they have to suffer through some periods of repressing their sexual desires. That'll teach them self-control,* she thought.

Rachel bit her bottom lip and looked down at her book, sighing wistfully. She closed her book—she could not concentrate. She scanned the airplane and all the movement within. She was amused by the bustle she noticed in the coach section in front of her. Adolescents were moving around, smiling, whispering, and enthusiastically flirting. Boys hung over the seats, vying for a word with the long-haired girls in tight tank tops. The girls sported more bare flesh than babies on a summer day—their spaghetti-strapped tops clung to their curves, exposing shoulders, cleavage, and midsections with belly rings. They flashed their form-fitting pants, mostly designer jeans with assorted tears, stripes, sparkles, and embroidery, at frequent intervals as they leaned over seats to whisper to their friends.

These girls, like their clothes, reflected tinges of exhibition-ism—they were loud, brash, and clamoring for eyes to notice them. These girls were a stark contrast to many other females scattered throughout the plane: young Jewish and Muslim women who were modestly dressed—arms covered, heads wrapped in scarves, and legs enveloped in long skirts—and who were quietly talking, reading, or sleeping. Rachel felt an affinity with these young women. Standing in line for the bathroom, she talked with some of them, and they seemed practical and sincere, yet warm. They reminded Rachel of the type that used to be called peasants. When she asked them about their backgrounds, these carefully dressed, modest, poised young women often revealed that they were raised by middle-class professional parents who practiced religious orthodoxy.

As she walked back to her seat, Rachel thought, *Funny how people assume that conservative women don't have sex. If they just counted their babies, they could guess that these women were getting and giving lots of sex.*

Rachel sat down in her window seat and thought, "Here I am, on my way to Israel." She did not smile at that thought. She had decided six months ago on her forty-fifth birthday that it was time to visit the Holy Land. She looked forward to seeing the famous land of Israel but at the same time felt a sense of dread about her visit. *I am not a Christian pilgrim. What am I?* Rachel wondered. Lately, she just felt tired of everything … tired of working, tired of waiting for the right man, tired of hoping that her daughter would respond to her phone calls, e-mails, or letters, tired of thinking about her traumatic past. Life seemed full of meaningless drudgery, full of obligations, full of getting up early, commuting, working with people that she just tolerated and clients that were hardly tolerable, coming home to a quiet house full of more work—cooking, cleaning, laundry. It was all too tiring. She wished for the energy and vigor of her youth, when she bounded out of bed and was excited about what the day might bring. Nowadays, she would rather sleep in on the weekend and shuffle around her house in slippers and pajamas. She hoped her trip to Israel would breathe new life into her stale, gray days.

Because Rachel had a seat in the middle of coach class, she had full view of the non-stop action of the adolescents. Rachel scanned the frenetic group of young people and noticed numerous Western-dressed adolescents on the plane who were quieter and less flamboyant. They were blocking out the world with headphones, connected to their own private musical or video world. She noticed some of the quiet ones sending surreptitious looks toward the adolescent commotion. They flashed looks of longing, as if they, too, wanted to brandish frenzied adolescent freedom and be part of the fiery exchanges of exuberance and flirtatious attention-seeking. Rachel recalled her own adolescent years, when she longed to speak and act freely. She had always vented her frustration in written words, allowing her to maintain privacy while expressing herself freely. *Undoubtedly these silent, longing ones understand that the freedom of the adolescent herd is the liberty to be as loud, foolish, and outrageous as possible. This does not match their character. But they sit there, awkwardly craving attention. I don't envy them*, she thought.

For most of her life, Rachel had longed for a different kind of freedom, a mental freedom. She had always been too interested in thoughts and ideas to act wildly, without inhibitions, except maybe when she was three years old. Rachel imagined how she would be if she was fifteen years old today. *I would probably be like one of the adolescents choosing an electronic shell of music or videos,* she thought. When she was a teenager, she had sought refuge in the shell of books. Her family life was chaotic, but books brought her peace. Books lit up her imagination more than music and took her on journeys that she thought that she could or would never take. She was enthralled with the ability of books to introduce her to the distilled extract of others' thought processes through written words. It was much easier to read a book than to try to participate in the tense, awkward conversations at the dinner table.

Rachel's social life was fragile when she was growing up, not just because she was fascinated by books and knowledge but because she preferred the company of adults. She was pulled more toward adults, because the adults had ideas and opinions that were interesting to hear. Ideas were always a lot more interesting to her than who was kissing whom, who was mad at whom, and who was dating whom.

Many of her peers alienated Rachel by making fun of her glasses and braces, her interest in science, her endless questions and curiosity, and her profound awkwardness around boys. As a protest against such a cruel milieu, she refused to follow her peer's fashion trends. Even in her youth, their styles of dress typically involved exposing as much flesh in public as legally possible. But Rachel did not care about which brands of jeans, purses, and shoes were "the best," partly because she thought it was ludicrous to spend so much money on a brand. She remembered thinking that being in the in-group was nothing but an empty status symbol. *Why would I want to be a part of a group of people who create expensive, empty hype over a piece of cotton that was made for fifty cents in Bangladesh? They are the fools.*

Many girls in her grade rejected other girls by rolling their eyes and turning their backs to them in the school corridors. *They were practicing emotional cruelty even then. I bet they have great lives now.* She chuckled sarcastically. *And probably they are still that way—always gossiping, being critical and negative about other people, hurting people intentionally.* But Rachel had liked to talk with adults, so the girls did not have much gossip fodder to use against her. And Rachel hadn't been on the cruel boys' radar either. Her shyness toward guys had served her well, making her invisible to them.

In high school, Rachel made a few close friends who were more intellectually progressive and more interested in the greater world than in the gossip about who was dating whom. Rachel and her friends joined Amnesty International and wrote letters to imprisoned prisoners of conscience. They collected canned goods in their neighborhood to donate to the food bank and then helped deliver boxes of food to the elderly and people with disabilities who could not go outside. After every delivery, the young people sat for a few minutes and talked about the weather, food, families, and news. By the time they left, the recipients were so grateful that they would start crying—over a few moments of talk. When she saw the power of the spoken word to affect people, Rachel decided to become a therapist. Her sex therapist specialty arose later, after she experienced life, love, and the cycles of relationships.

Rachel imagined that if she could redo her past, she would not change much, except being less shy around guys, so that she actually could speak to them at dances. *I was not hip back in high school, and I certainly would not be so now, if I was an adolescent today.* Rachel thought about getting married after finishing college and how happy she was during that time. But she realized she'd never quite believed that someone wanted to marry her and be with her forever. She'd never expected that. *I loved him excitedly and intensely because he had decided to love me.*

Rachel thought, *Adults make one big mistake—they don't tell you growing up that girls like me have just as good a chance of getting married as any blond high school cheerleader! Adults had tried to encourage girls like me by citing the allegory of the ugly duckling becoming a beautiful swan. But they did not think about what they were saying! That implied that I was ugly and that in the end beauty was still important for keeping a man's love.*

I know that is a Big Lie because some of my most sexually active clients, those who have beautiful, solid sexual relationships with their spouses, are average-looking and dress professionally in public. Their private love for each other frees them in their sexual expression. And they report enjoying their sexual encounters with their spouse immensely. I know from my therapy practice that the "beautiful" people are often the most self-conscious and hold back in bed. Funny how many people assume that you have to be beautiful to have and enjoy sex.

chapter 8

MEN ARE PULLED OUT from between women's legs as newborns, and there they want to return for all of their lives. King Solomon was no exception.

King Solomon looked up from the scrolls of the temple, casting his glance beyond the ring of advisors and planners, fixating on the gentle flow of a woman's garment as she strode toward the fountain. Her garment, obviously made of the finest linen, shimmered and floated with the westward breeze. Her braided hair peeked slightly from under her veil. This signaled to Solomon that she was a modern woman who did not rigidly follow religious rules, because women were required to cover all of their hair in front of men who were not part of their family.

Her golden hair was Solomon's favorite type. The brief, intense look directly into his eyes told him all he needed to know. He licked his lips and then wiped them with the back of his hand, as if to remove the desert dust. His body had sounded the alarm, and he knew that he could only contain it for a short time before it would become too painful to bear. It would cause a low buzz in his ears. When that happened, he could not quite hear others talking, nor could he concentrate on their words until he relieved the sexual pressure.

He halted his meeting, excused himself from his advisors, and hurriedly walked toward the fountain so he could exert his royal charms on the woman. He quickly glanced back at the group and saw that the advisors did not appear to react to his quick departure, nor did they show any suspicion about his reason for leaving. But the men were huddled over the blueprints, so King Solomon was not able to see the suppressed smiles of four of his six advisors or the glances of the other two. They knew.

Women gravitated toward King Solomon for a variety of reasons. The most common was the financial power he wielded, because of the tax money he received from his people. Once he took a woman as a concubine or mistress, the woman would be his property for life and would be added to his women's quarters. There she would live in luxury, wear beautifully woven and embroidered linen dresses, and eat deliciously prepared foods. If she continued as his lover, he would occasionally give her expensive gifts, such as pearl necklaces or gold earrings.

If a woman was able to catch Solomon's eye, even for one night, an undeniable social security resulted. King Solomon did not discard his women, even if his passion only lasted a short interlude of a few hours or one night, because there was a high possibility that the woman may become pregnant with his child. Solomon extravagantly took care of his own. So women were not afraid of pursuing or seducing him as a lover.

The competition among the many women of Solomon's clan was intense. The only requirement to join the club was the ability to attract Solomon, based on his current moods and needs. Because of the great rivalry among the women to be Solomon's favorite, the issue for Solomon's women became the ability to continue to seduce him after the first time as his lover. The secrets related to obtaining the coveted position as his favorite woman were highly guarded and never discussed among the women in the women's quarters. Many of the women aspired to be his "most beloved," which meant becoming the Queen of Israel.

Most of the women who joined Solomon's women's quarters came from poor families, unable to provide marriage dowries. The lack of a dowry was not an issue for any of Solomon's women. If he liked a woman, he did not need her money, and he would generously share some of his fortune with each woman. Most families considered it an honor when Solomon chose their daughter to be a part of his royal palace. They could never refuse, knowing what security it would bring to their daughter. The families did not talk about the dozens of other women in a similar position to their daughter, nor did they view being chosen as unseemly or as slavery. Solomon could offer their daughter a style of living that she could otherwise never obtain, given that most of the population lived in poverty.

The gossip about King Solomon was that he preferred a woman from a poor family. He liked to save women from a bitter, hard life. And the women who were born into poor households treated him as he wanted. These poor women were not only overwhelmed by his grandeur and power, but they were so grateful for his generosity that they were silent and subservient toward Solomon whenever he came to them. They were afraid of speaking to him. He did not seem to notice as long as he got what he wanted from them.

King Solomon did not marry all of his lovers and mistresses. At first, he thought marrying a woman and then having sex was the honorable thing to do. But as the years passed and the number of his wives swelled into the hundreds, he saw no reason to continue marrying all the women he had sex with. But he pledged to still take care of them for the rest of their lives in a separate house, the women's quarters.

However strongly attracted Solomon was to a new woman, he eventually became bored with her. His lover usually provided no conversation, no imagination, just a physical connection and brief comfort. This was especially true with the women who were afraid of Solomon, too afraid to even speak in his presence. The intangible force that brought them together vanished like "smoke in the wind," as Solomon used to say.

After Solomon had plumbed the depths of a woman's body and soul, he would often become bored and withdraw from her, no longer interested in trying to bridge the chasm between two people via the fleshly bridge. Once Solomon was tired of a woman, he was no longer hungry for her company. And his anger would creep into his bed and pollute the room. Of course, his abrupt change toward her would confuse and upset the woman. His advisors knew to look for this change in Solomon. When they saw anger in his eyes in the morning, they would come in and escort the shaken woman to the women's quarters.

The more time Solomon spent with various women, the more he understood that behind their cloak of beauty lay emptiness, terror, and weakness. The longer he stayed with one woman, the more he sensed that void. This frightened him and made him reject her with anger and contempt. Her sobbing and wailing over his rejection of her did not affect him. He wanted her to go away from him. Solomon did not see that the woman was giving him everything she had that she could give to him. He wanted to crave and possess her, not to be repelled by her.

Solomon sought a woman who could teach him something. He wanted a woman who was not awkward around him, a woman who could explain the unknown to him. Instead, he met walls of silence and nothingness in the women he probed. He quickly found the edge of the person—the border of her knowledge, the end of her being. But Solomon kept seeking answers, looking behind every owner of beautiful eyes and long, shiny hair who came across his path.

Each of Solomon's lovers did not expect him to reject her,

although each knew that he typically did so to other women. Her own private opinion was that *she* alone could make him happy where others had failed. So when Solomon inevitably sent a woman to the women's quarters, she cried out of shock and grief, unprepared. The women in the house called the journey when a woman walked to the women's quarters for the first time the "trail of tears." After mourning for a few weeks or a few months, the rejected woman would change. She would either become aggressive, competing with the other women in the house to return to Solomon, or she would curl up into a tight ball and cling to the wall of the women's quarters all day long.

It took some creative, daring moves for a woman to be allowed to return to Solomon, for he had a continuous supply of willing women waiting for him outside the palace and throughout the land. So the women of Solomon's house would experiment with Egyptian-style makeup, clothing, and hair designs in order to catch his eye at their weekly Sabbath meals, an event that all of his women and children attended. Some tried to eliminate competition through gossip and by spreading lies that certain women had lovers on the outside. The only way to leave or be thrown out of Solomon's women's quarters was having an outside lover.

Not all women tried to seduce Solomon; some did the opposite. Some would try to hide from him because they wanted to leave the quarters and marry a man in the community. If a woman's family was willing to arrange a marriage to a good match, she could escape from Solomon's women's quarters. But many families did not do that, because the parents of the daughter looked forward to bragging rights for having a grandchild born of King Solomon and a daughter who was protected and sustained by a wealthy man.

Several women a year left the women's quarters to marry men from their home villages. For the most part, Solomon let them go and gave them a small bag of gold and his blessings. Some of the women's families did not want them to return home because all the neighbors knew that the daughter lived at Solomon's palace. The families believed that if their daughter returned home, it was because King Solomon had rejected her, even if it had been her choice to leave.

Some women who wanted to leave Solomon's women's quarters had problems trying to marry another man, because all the men knew that the women who returned from Solomon's palace were no longer virgins. But many men secretly viewed the women who wanted to leave Solomon's palace as very desirable and good marriage candidates, because those women had associated with King Solomon. "If the powerful king desired the woman, then she must indeed be very worthy and very beautiful!" the men exclaimed.

chapter 9

As THE STREETS OF the Old City in Jerusalem started closing for the Sabbath, Sarah and Moshe zipped down the street in Moshe's red 1993 Honda sedan. The warmth of the sunset reflected off Jerusalem's limestone architecture, making the city glow in a peculiar way. Most travelers noticed Jerusalem's special glow, often attributing it to the spiritual forces in Jerusalem and not to the particular components of its architecture. For centuries, Christians have sung the hymn, "Jerusalem the golden, the city of the blessed."

But when Christians visit the City of the Blessed, they see the dirty buses belching out diesel fumes, trash in the streets, stores and markets everywhere, soldiers with guns whistling at the women in short skirts and tight tank tops, taxi cab drivers yelling at each other and honking at potential customers, and hoards of thin stray alley cats jumping out of dumpsters, roaming the streets for food, and competing with the rats for a scrap of food. The Christian tourists stand paralyzed, their Nikon cameras around their necks, wearing their tan parachute pants and white sneakers. They feel duped by the religious stories they were told growing up. "This is not the storybook version of Jerusalem! This is not the Land of Milk and Honey!" they protest to their tour guide as they helplessly stand by their tour bus, stunned by their disillusionment. "It looks more like the Land of Dust and Bitterness!" one elderly woman yelled to her tour guide.

Christians' experience with the Real Israel is like when young people go crazy over the idea of holding a cute little cherubic face in their arms, not realizing what it means to have ten wet and smelly diapers a day to change and a little one who cries off and on all day. They fall in love with the idea, which is enough to get them to pursue the dream and ignore the dirty, difficult reality of raising a child. Of course, they mutter, "What was I thinking? What have I gotten into?" after the fifth night of three hours of sleep, when their child is howling in pain with a stomach ache. But as proud parents, they will forget their exhaustion in a day or two and tell their neighbors and friends that their child is the most beautiful in the world.

This is just how Christians react to Jerusalem. They fall in love with the idea of Jerusalem during church services and Bible schools. Their excitement about visiting the Holy Land continues through the time when they step out of the plane at Ben Gurion International airport and take the shuttle to Jerusalem. When they step into Jerusalem's streets, they recoil against the onslaught of angry taxi drivers, earsplitting traffic jams, diesel buses polluting the air, muggy, hot weather, aggressive shopkeepers, rude pedestrians, and dirty streets. They stare numbly at the modern, raucous life of Jerusalem, wondering why they had such different visions of Jerusalem. Everything they have ever heard about Jerusalem was about peace and spirituality, from the time that they attended Bible school to when they signed up for the trip with their own ministers, who sold them a tour package.

But after a few days of visits to religious places, some prayer services, and good Middle Eastern food, they no longer perceive the smell and the dirt. Once again, they proudly crown Jerusalem the spiritual queen of cities.

Despite the glow of the sunset and the gold glint of the Dome of the Rock, there was silence, a rather stony one, within Moshe's car. Sarah and Moshe's next argument had been triggered, like most romantic conflicts, by a miscommunication. One party thought the point was minor, while the other party believed the point was headline news. One party was jocular, trying to alter the mood by lightheartedly changing the subject, while the other party dug their heels in deeper, becoming angry at the attempt at comic relief. The joking, of course, was interpreted as minimizing and avoiding the issue at hand by the other party.

Sarah: "What did you mean by saying that I was high maintenance? What am I, a car?"

Moshe: "Well, you know cars need tune-ups and oil changes every few months ...like maybe a tune-up of your tone of voice toward me right now."

Sarah: "What do you mean, tone of voice? What am I, a child who must obey you?"

Moshe: "Well, that would be nice sometimes."

Sarah: "What—are you saying that you are not happy with me? That you don't love me?"

Moshe was quiet for a moment, holding his breath. He felt his stomach tighten and a glimmer of pain from his ulcer. He knew that if he said nothing more to her, it would enrage her further. So he brought up the only thing that he knew would zoom to her very core. "Sarah, I gave you a promise ring, didn't I?"

He looked over at her and saw her bite her lip. Her eyes glistened. He knew that his missile had hit the target—a direct hit this time. Sarah was silent, pensively looking out of the window. Moshe suddenly noticed the glow of Jerusalem at sunset and the way the limestone throughout the city reflected the dwindling sun, creating a warm, yellow hue that radiated, as if a vibrating color encircled the city. Moshe thought, *Damn, how I love this city.*

After a few minutes, Sarah whispered pleadingly, "*Metuka,* you are good for me. Don't leave me." She said this while hanging on to his right arm, her forehead pressed into his cotton shirt, which stretched over tight, army-toned muscles.

Moshe sat up straight and tried to hold back his grin. "No, no, my dear, I will never do that," he said. And she smiled triumphantly as they sped down Ben Yehuda Street toward his parents' house.

On the surface, Moshe's parents seemed like a typical middle-age, middle-class couple, with two grown children, expectations of upcoming grandchildren, and no other hopes for their futures except to have enough money to retire soon and to avoid becoming disabled. Both emigrated from Russia to Israel in 1935, when it was still called Palestine and was being run by the British. Moshe's parents worked long hours every day in their early years of marriage in order to raise two boisterous boys who seemed to have endless energy, especially at night, when they would try to get them to stay in a bed and actually sleep. Instead, the boys seemed to have a repeat button. They kept jumping out of bed and asking for water or milk or why the sky was blue.

Moshe's mother, Mariva, had hair that was dyed red and a body that was sturdy like a Russian peasant. Mariva used to say that raising her two boys made her age a few decades prematurely. Moshe's father, Benjamin, was a quiet man with a glistening bald spot on his head and reading glasses like Trotsky. He loved to read books, newspapers, and academic journals. He viewed reading magazines as a waste of his time. And all romantic novels and poetry were an embarrassment to Benjamin. The plot had to be substantial, analyzable, and linear, like a good mystery. Otherwise he thought the writing was as rotten as mildewed tomatoes.

Despite his love of learning, Benjamin could not talk with

his wife without sounding irritated. He was always in a hurry to finish the conversation and return to what he was doing. Mariva quickly responded to his terse words with sharp speech and annoyed looks. She would pursue him into his study to try to get a decision out of him about tonight's dinner, tomorrow's meeting with friends, or the weekend plans. But he would claim that he did not like to plan ahead and would decide later, after he had finished his work. She kept pressing him to tell her now, so that she could make plans. He kept refusing, asking her to leave so that he could work on his research paper to advance his university position. She would stand in the doorway of his office, waiting for some information from him and would only leave after she had received some, even though he never told her his final decision, nor his feelings on the matter. Mariva would leave, feeling triumphant and empowered. But Benjamin smiled, knowing that he would change his viewpoint in the near future, just to show her who was in control.

When Moshe and Sarah arrived, Benjamin and Mariva, after quickly greeting Moshe and Sarah at the door, continued bickering for several minutes. It was as if the momentum of their verbal warfare was too great for Mariva and Benjamin to control, making them forget that other people were in the room as they continued arguing over certain facts. Instead of making the guests feel comfortable, they handed them a drink and continued their marital squabble. After all, they seemed to think that it only was their son and his girlfriend, who had visited their home many times over the past few months. They seemed to feel that there was no need to hide anything. In fact, they relished knowing that Moshe would try to understand the conflict, that each would be able to give Moshe his or her side of the story, and that Moshe would always try to intervene with the diplomacy of United Nations' blue hats. They expected that their son would enter into the diatribe to save them from each other.

Tonight was no different from any other night in their game of verbal sparring. But when Moshe stepped over the threshold and greeted his parents, he walked over to the TV and turned it up loudly. He knew after the first few sentences and from their facial expressions that his parents had been arguing. If he became involved, the ulcer throbbing in his gut would hurt even more than it already did. He wanted the arguing to stop, but he knew that saying anything was of no use. Any pleas for them to cease the edgy discourse would be ignored. It was their habit to treat each other this way, and it was more important for each of them to achieve verbal superiority over their spouse than it was to suppress the conflict for the sake of their son and his girlfriend. To Sarah, all was normal with Moshe's parents, for it was similar to how her parents treated each other.

After a few minutes, Benjamin and Mariva reached a stalemate, and then they warily eyed each other as they ran over to greet Sarah warmly, hugging her and kissing her on the cheeks. They talked over each other with questions about Sarah, Sarah's parents, Sarah's job, and Sarah's health. Benjamin and Mariva talked louder and louder, interrupting each other. It was as if they each wanted to display greater hospitality to Sarah than the other.

"Sarah, my darling, it looks like you have lost weight!" Mariva said.

"You are always as lovely as a desert bloom!" Benjamin exclaimed.

"How are your parents, my dear?" Mariva asked.

"How is your apartment in Tel Aviv?" Benjamin inquired.

"Are you eating enough? You look thin," Mariva proclaimed.

"How's your job?" Benjamin asked.

Sarah responded in half-sentences to one parent before the other parent intervened with a new question. Moshe stood at the TV and watched over the noise of the news broadcast. He did not say a word. Moshe thought about all of the embarrassment, stress, frustration, and anguish that these arguments had brought him in his childhood years. He tried to avoid his parents' mind games. He did not want to be a mediator between his parents. *I'm not a family therapist. And I do not want such a role,* he thought. So he turned to his parents and screamed, "Silence!" and then turned up the TV.

Sarah, Mariva, and Benjamin froze and looked at Moshe with utter disbelief. His one word hung silently in the room, and their lips stiffened, as if all power to speak was lost.

chapter 10

SITTING OUTSIDE IN A café on Arlozorov Street in Tel Aviv, Rachel's contemplative musing over a coffee was disturbed by a group of kids down the street pushing past each other and laughing loudly. Their boisterous laughter made her more glum and depressed. She was tired of her heaviness, her fatigue, and her obsession—her annoying obsession—over Mr. Hit-and-Run, a man thousands of miles away from her both physically and mentally. She had wanted him for a very long time, and she got mixed signals from him. What made the situation worse was the fact that he was married. It took Rachel about one year after meeting Mr. Hit-and-Run to discover that he was married. He did not wear a wedding ring. But after realizing that there seemed to be mutual attraction, Rachel began looking for personal information about him on the Internet and found out that he had a wife. She was stunned. She thought it was unusual that he had not mentioned his family during the whole year. *Maybe that meant that he was unhappy with his marital life*, she wondered. *Does his interest in me mean that he is about to change his personal circumstances, that I should wait for him?*

When Rachel saw him at work, she often thought, *My heart wants to make love to you, but my mind says, 'I will not commit adultery. I will not!'* She always tried to act and dress in a professional manner at work, never intentionally publicizing her large breasts or her long, slender legs. Rachel knew her breasts were large by men's standards, but she never flaunted them. They were a secret surprise tucked away in the folds of her clothes. But when she took off her suit jacket, the outline of her curvy silhouette was noticeable. The first time she did that, Mr. Hit-and-Run looked stunned, staring at her breasts as if he was shocked to find a hidden treasure. From that moment, whenever they talked, Mr. Hit-and-Run's eyes would slowly sink down to the folds of her clothes and linger at chest level with hunger. *Even under layers of clothes and a suit, he is imagining how big there are.* Rachel smirked. *He looks like he could devour me and yank my breasts out of their cradle and take possession of them like a squatter moving into an abandoned house. He's like a tinderbox of repressed desire waiting to explode!*

So he wants me. But what do I do with that? she thought. *What is he thinking? He doesn't seem to want what I want yet—a passionate, exclusive relationship. That means not being married to someone else while being with me. But maybe he plans to divorce and remarry someday?* But the questions she asked herself were of little use. He said nothing to her on a personal level, except for a cleverly disguised sexual joke. Whenever Mr. Hit-and-Run was around Rachel for any length of time, he started getting restless and looked ready to bolt, like a wild horse challenging the reins. At first, Rachel thought that it was because he disliked being around her. But he always came back to her, seeking her out.

Despite knowing that he was married and despite her own pledge not to commit adultery, she did not want to stop talking with him. She wanted to tell him everything. She knew she was hooked on communicating with him. She'd had several sexual relationships before when communication was mostly about sex. She willingly participated in that talk but then tired of it, knowing that it was only talk to seduce and add heat, not for drawing them closer to each other. It felt superficial, not like real communication. It felt downright cheesy. *No doubt sex is a form of non-verbal communication. But any clown can say fantasy phrases to fuel the fire, like "You are so hot" and "You really turn me on." That doesn't mean you actually like and trust your partner. You're just cranking them up! "Do me" is not a deep sharing of the soul, but sex-fueled talk!* Rachel stared blankly at the newspaper on her café table.

Her interactions with Mr. Hit-and-Run always made her extremely chatty, even giddy. She wanted to share all of her feelings, emotions, and deeper thoughts with him, to hold nothing back. She kept whispering to herself in the mirror every night, "I do not want to commit adultery. He's married. I fear God and man's fury if I commit adultery."

She started looking for another job when she could no longer take the sexual tension between them. *I think adultery is for cowards who are afraid to speak up and possibly disappoint a few people,* she thought heatedly as she remembered those days of longing and unfulfilled desire.

In her private practice, she counseled many heartbroken women who came into her office for therapy after their husbands had cheated on them. She explained some of the dynamics of affairs to them. "Some people like to have affairs while they are married, because there is no threat of change, no pressure to be serious, unless they are caught, which of course they never expect to be. They never think that their illicit sex partner may want to force them into a choice by leaving little lacy items around, hoping that his wife would find them. But you know, placing a G-string in the man's suit pocket is one of the favorite tricks of mistresses of married men."

Most women clients protested at Rachel's comments, claiming that their guy wanted to marry them. They claimed that once their married lover got a divorce and then married them, everything would be all right. She responded gently to those depressed and angry women. "You forget that you're loving a man who cannot be trusted in intimate issues. He is cheating on his wife now. If you ever became his wife, he can cheat on you too." They often snapped back at her, "No, if he loved me, he would never do such a thing to me!" Rachel gently replied, "Well, maybe he is doing that to you right now—cheating on you with his wife!" That response often made them cry.

Rachel never intended to fall in love with Mr. Hit-and-Run, especially after discovering that he was married. But it did happen, strongly, deeply, possessively, jealously. She started craving communication with him. It crept up slowly, like a natural gas leak, silent but lethal. Whenever she was apart from him, she would daydream about him, wondering what he was doing and whether he was anxious to see her. One day, out of frustration, she wrote a cynical poem using a male voice:

> Give me your emotional strokes:
> I like your jealousy.
> I am here, but
> You cannot have me.
> I'm in a relationship
> But keep giving me
> Your attention
> While I taunt you
> And then run away scared.

In March one fateful year, Rachel and Mr. Hit-and-Run attended a professional conference together. They went into a presentation together and then out to dinner with other colleagues. Under the table, she could feel his knee rubbing up against her leg. She moved her leg back because there were other people at the table, but she glanced at him from the corner of her eye. He was not looking at her but at his food. She thought that the knee contact might be accidental. But then it happened again. His legged collided with hers, jiggling in an anxious way. Again, no eye contact. She moved her leg back. *What kind of game is this?* she thought.

After dinner, a group of colleagues wandered back to their conference hotels. Mr. Hit-and-Run dashed ahead of the crowd up the steps and then held the elevator open. When Rachel was the only one to enter, he pressed the buttons nervously. She looked at him. *What was he so afraid of?* There was awkward silence until Rachel asked him what he was planning on doing tomorrow. He looked warily at her with a side-long glance, a colt ready to bolt.

Rachel longed to touch him, to comfort him, to feel his muscles, his strength, his power. But her nightly incantation, "I will not commit adultery," rang in her head, so she did not move an inch closer to him. Instead, she gripped tightly to the handrail in the elevator. She felt very self-conscious standing there, trying to talk to him. The elevator doors opened, and she started stepping out. He put out his hand, brushing hers, and signaled to the floor level. "One more," he said. He started punching the elevator buttons again. She laughed uneasily and stepped back into the elevator.

Rachel leaned back against the side of the elevator and looked at him. *It's not going to happen tonight*, she thought. She wanted to tear his clothes off and kiss him all over. She could not concentrate or talk. The silence was tense and awkward. The elevator beeped, and he said, "Here it is." He took off, throwing a quick "Good night" over his shoulder as he ran down the hallway in front of her. But then he stopped in the middle of hallway, turned around, and looked at her strangely.

The next morning, she wondered if it was a dream or if it was indeed a memory as she stroked her lip softly in front of the mirror.

chapter 11

Moshe's parents, Mariva and Benjamin, were ecstatic to receive his phone call one evening about ten o'clock with "the big news." "I am getting married, Ima!" he excitedly told his mother.

A hundred questions descended upon Moshe. Where? When? How? And finally it came to the question, "Why are you telling us this by phone? Why didn't you come here so we can hug you and toast your happiness?" Mariva became enraged. "Is this all that I get, for all the years of love and sweat? *Ma zeh?* What are you doing to your mother?" She flung the phone to Benjamin, who picked it up off the floor and heartily said, "Congratulations, my son. Don't worry, she is just overexcited right now." They talked a little about Moshe's evening and then switched to the latest soccer triumph by a Jerusalem team.

When Benjamin hung up the phone, he walked to the bedroom door and stood there, looking at his sobbing wife, who was rolled up in the bed cover, tissues strewn across the floor and mattress.

"Mariva, what's wrong?" he calmly asked.

"How can you be so calm when our only son has excluded us from his life? From one of the most important moments of his life?"

"Mariva, that's not true. He called us to tell us the news."

"Yes, but it was three hours after the fact."

Benjamin shrugged his shoulders and fell silent. He was thinking that Moshe and Sarah probably ran home from the restaurant after she accepted his proposal and made passionate love. *That's what I would have done if Sarah had said yes to me,* he mused.

Mariva saw him smile wryly and then yelled, "Oh my God! You have someone else! You are sleeping with someone else, aren't you? You are planning to divorce me, aren't you?"

"No, I am not having sex with someone else. I am not even having sex with you. But you are right. I do want a divorce. I want a divorce so I can have peace in my life. You yell about everything, and suspect me of many things that I have never done. Things that maybe I will do if I'm done with you, and I won't be ashamed, nor fear any wrath from you. You are absolutely right, for once. I do want a divorce! Thank you for helping me to realize that." Benjamin turned around and headed toward the kitchen, where he grabbed a Coca-Cola and walked out the door.

Mariva sat up on the disheveled bed and stared, transfixed, at the closed front door.

Moshe and Sarah decided to visit her parents, not Mariva and Benjamin, for the Sabbath. There were a few guests and three siblings, which made for a lively evening of singing, talking, gossiping, and laughing. The apartment was small, with three bedrooms that had cheap plastic doors, a combined living and dining room with a large table in the center, worn, dirty couches, and a cramped, busy kitchen with no room for a table. But the porch was the best feature, the reason her parents never moved after Sarah and her two siblings moved out to live in their own apartments. The porch overlooked the cityscape, a panoramic view of Haifa. Its soft white lights twinkled and shimmered, especially at night during the summer when the invisible wafts of heat from the desert floor blanketed the air.

Their porch had offered an overlook for many historic moments—the wars, the bombings, the air raids, and the post-war celebrations. More recently, weekly suicide bombs and the ensuing medical and police responses to the emergency lit up the night sky with a cluster of blinking lights for hours after the act of self-immolation was over.

When it came time for sleep, Sarah's father warily eyed Moshe and motioned to the futon in the living room. "You may sleep here, or in your car," he said with a smirk and a wink. They both grinned widely, because both knew that Moshe and Sarah had been living together for months. "My wife tells me we have rules in this house that you must respect," he laughingly said, and then he threw Moshe and pillow and a blanket.

Sarah's parents had met and married later in life in America, where they both had immigrated as children. After growing up in carefree America, they joined the radical Zionist movement and "made *ayilah*," or immigrated, to Haifa when Sarah was an adolescent. This meant that their religious outlook was more old-fashioned than most of the parents of Sarah's friends. Many of Sarah's girlfriends were living with their boyfriends and were not very interested in getting married, as often is the case with children of divorced parents. Sarah's friends preferred living together with their boyfriends and having a "we shall see" attitude. They never talked about the subject of marriage directly with their boyfriends. They explained this approach to their parents and relatives: "It'll scare him away if I bring up marriage."

But paradoxically, Sarah's girlfriends waited anxiously for the proposal and the ring, while telling each other, "I can always find another if this does not work out." The girls knew that they had a lot of power in the relationship—sexual and procreative power. They had sex with their boyfriends whenever they wanted, but they still talked about weddings, read women's magazines about how to get their boyfriends to propose to them, and fantasized about getting a large diamond ring as a holiday surprise. They talked about how they would throw a big party, buy a white, tasteful, but sexy and revealing wedding dress, and plan a tropical honeymoon.

And of course, Sarah would not admit to her friends that she, too, secretly wanted to be the glamorous center of attention and envy of all women and girls for at least one day of her life. She also imagined stacks of wedding gifts, wrapped in silver and gold ribbons, and dozens of large checks given to her as wedding gifts. *A wedding is the ultimate fulfillment as a woman, even more than having a child, because I can easily have a child without a wedding,* Sarah thought. *A wedding is the path to the ultimate social status. It means that I'm wanted, desired, loved, supported, and singled out over all other women,* she mused. "It'll be all about me for that day," she declared to herself, "so I must have a wedding!"

Sarah remembered that it took Moshe several tries to propose to her. She explained to her single girlfriends, "Most men like the free ride of sex without commitment. But most women are turned on by a guy's commitment. When the girlfriend threatens for the twentieth time to leave if he does not commit, he eventually realizes that he likes what he has and that she's ready and willing to say yes to him. So he starts fearing that he will lose her and stops fearing that she will reject him. After all, there is nothing worse to a man than a woman refusing to marry him when he asks. And he runs out to buy the ring and seal the deal. And that is exactly what happened between Moshe and me." Her girlfriends gasped at her maturity and insight and then bombarded her with questions about how they could get their boyfriends to commit. *Maybe I should write a book about this?* Sarah thought.

Even though Sarah was a transplant from America, she was similar to the "normal" secular girls in Israel. She lived with a boyfriend at age sixteen and then another one at twenty-one. Then, at age twenty-three, she met Moshe. He resisted her sexual advances when he visited her at her Dizengoff Street apartment on their first date, two days after meeting at a party. He was curious, though, and asked her to a second dinner date the next evening. By the third evening, they were having sex in her apartment. By week five, she asked him to move into her apartment.

Moshe thought her old-school parents would never forgive him if he and Sarah moved in together. Moshe was harassed by his friends about this, and Sarah had many long talks with her girlfriends, analyzing his level of commitment, his possible fear of a relationship, and his feelings of guilt about sex. They had many fights over this matter. Moshe thought it would finally be resolved once he gave her an engagement ring. He proposed to her one night. Things did change, but not as he wanted or expected them to.

Sarah started flirting even more with other men after she got the ring—or at least that was what Moshe thought. Her girlfriends claimed that he was jealous and possessive because he had formalized their relationship and mapped out their future together.

Moshe told his friends that he saw Sarah smile warmly toward another man at the coffee shop, and at the waiter at the restaurant and the half-naked men playing ball on the Tel Aviv beach. He thought she enjoyed the attention men gave her over her svelte figure in the tight tank top and jeans and her braided blond hair a little too much. He also thought she talked too much about the male movie stars in the films they saw together and showed too much interest in the personal lives of the guys she worked with.

Moshe did not know what to do. He did not think he needed to see a psychotherapist, because he thought that he had some level of proof, of data, of real observations. "Sarah needs to change, not me!" he said angrily to his three friends as they played racquetball. "But I will not say anything to Sarah because she will claim that I am too paranoid and suspicious. I know she will say that!" He hit the ball hard against the wall, and it flew past his ear. His friends tried to calm him, saying that it was all in his imagination.

"But how can I trust her, my future wife? She keeps talking, talking, talking all the time to different men!" Moshe said. "After all, that is how we met—we started talking at a coffee shop in Tel Aviv, waiting for our cappuccinos. She can do that again when I am not around." His friends again tried to convince him that he was just nervous because he was engaged. "If she started having sex that quickly with me," Moshe yelled at them, "then she can move that quickly with other men too." He dropped his racquet and walked off the court, slamming the door behind him. His friends did not move. They looked at each other and shrugged. Then one yelled, "Let's play!" and hit the ball against the wall.

Moshe grabbed his cell phone, towel, and keys from his locker and walked out into the scorching Tel Aviv sun. *Sarah really wants to get married,* he thought, *but I don't think it matters to her who she marries, as long as it's a Jewish man who can earn a lot of money.* He spat on the ground. *I feel replaceable!* He imagined breaking off the engagement with her and then thought, *No! But one day she is going to step over that line and tell me it's over and good-bye, like she has done to so many other guys. Ring or no ring, she will do whatever the hell she wants.*

Moshe was scared. *I don't know what to do. I want her, and she wants me now. But I don't think she really wants me. She just wants a man to want and need her. She really does not want me. She wants arm candy to escort her to the movies, to parties, to dinners, and to friends' weddings. And she picked me because she knows I am safe and won't cheat on her.*

He paused at the stop light on Jabotinsky Street and looked the cars whizzing by, the people hurrying down the street. Nobody seemed to pay any attention to him. *What should I do? She pounced on me sexually and could not get enough of me in the beginning. But now it's all about pleasing her. And if I don't keep working hard to please her, I know that some rainy day when she is depressed and angry, she will walk out the door into another man's waiting arms. And lots of arms are waiting for Sarah right now. And she knows it. She walks around with extreme confidence about her looks and sexual desirability. She thinks she can have anyone she wants. If she throws me away, another man will take her place,* he thought angrily. He paid for his coffee and looked for a place to sit down in the crowded cafe.

Moshe saw a woman wearing a hajib sitting alone and drinking coffee. He noted that she was reading a book written by Rabbi Shmuley Boteach called *Kosher Sex*. About ten years ago, the book was talked about a lot in Israel. Many adolescent boys read it furtively at night and passed along copies to their friends when they were done.

"Can I share your table?"

"Sure, please," she said haltingly in Hebrew.

"That's okay. I speak English." He quickly smiled. "I'm Moshe," he said and reached out his hand to her. "I see the book you are reading. I've read it. But aren't you Muslim?" he asked.

"Yes, I'm Muslim. My name is Fatima. Nice to meet you." She grinned broadly as she responded in mispronounced Hebrew.

chapter 12

AFTER WANDERING THE STREETS of Jerusalem for two days, looking at Jewish styles and crafts on Ben Yehuda Street and the Mahne Yehuda market, Rachel decided that it was time to do what she had been thinking about for several dark years. She called up Julie, an American friend who worked for the International Red Cross/Red Crescent in Bethlehem. They exchange enthusiastic greetings and quick news about their lives. Soon the conversation slowed. After a long pause, Rachel said somberly to Julie, "It is time."

Julie replied, "Okay, I have been waiting for you. I will come pick you up after I get off work at three p.m." They exchanged information about Rachel's hotel.

Julie arrived in a dusty, gray Toyota that had seen a lot of miles and a few car accidents. Julie embraced Rachel softly and said in a sweet, nurturing voice, "So you are ready?" Rachel bit her lip and nodded. Julie took her hand and led her to the car, gently helping Rachel into the car. Rachel's face looked numb.

They drove in silence down narrow streets of Jerusalem, dodging and braking for the shoppers who acted like pedestrian crossings were only made for school children. As the limestone apartment buildings started to become sparser, Rachel started cringing and clinging to the handle of the car door. Her face was contorted, but she did not make any sound. When Julie saw the sign for Bethlehem, she pulled the car over.

"Do you want me to turn around, Rachel?" she said gently, stroking her on the shoulder.

"No, go on! Please!" Rachel gasped after saying those words, and then the tears erupted.

In her European accent, Julie softly said, "I know. I know it hurts. But you must face the memory so that it does not haunt you anymore."

Rachel wept silently as Julie slowly drove forward. She drove five blocks into the town and pulled over near a bus stop. She put on her hazard lights and then got out and walked to the right side of the car. She slowly opened the door and crouched beside Rachel. After a few moments, Julie said, "It is time to look up," and Rachel raised her head.

Through her veil of silent tears, Rachel looked at the empty bus stop. She looked at it, as if watching and listening for something. Then a deep moan started from within her chest, as if coming directly from her heart, her core, her soul, and traveled up through her throat and out her mouth as a moan that turned into a loud, "*Nooooo!*" People across the street looked over to the car and whipped out their cell phones and started yelling into them.

Julie tried to embrace Rachel through the noise and tears, but Rachel twisted away from her. Rachel bent over the dashboard and started hitting it with her fists. Within a minute, two police cars with sirens on pulled up behind and in front of the car. A woman police officer jumped out from the car in front, and a policeman ran from the car in back. Both ran to the driver's side of the car with their guns drawn.

They yelled at Julie in Hebrew. Julie raised her hands in the air while yelling back in broken Hebrew. Julie yelled, "This is a grieving mother who lost her sons in a terrorist attack here. Put down your guns." They lowered their weapons, looked at Julie, and then nodded.

Julie started gently pulling Rachel out of the car and helped her stand up. The police holstered their guns, and curious people started walking forward, asking them for information.

Julie and Rachel walked slowly to the bus stop that was ten feet away from the parked car. The closer they got, the more Rachel looked like her feet were made of lead. Rachel leaned on Julie, sobbing and trying to speak. Julie hugged her tightly and inched her forward.

Finally, they reached the bus stop. Julie waited for Rachel to lift her face. She kept stroking her hair and rubbing her arms. More people gathered nearby and talked quickly in Hebrew. Rachel slowly raised her head and then screamed, "Why God? Why?" and then burst out crying again. She dropped to the ground, pulling Julie down with her.

As they sat on the ground, ten men stepped forward. Most of them wore the black hats and suits of the Orthodox. They circled around the two women but did not touch them. They started chanting the Kaddish prayer of mourning. When the men finished their prayer, they stepped back from the circle.

Then the women who had been standing nearby put their shopping bags down and rushed in. They pressed in tightly, embracing Rachel and Julie, touching them on the head, the face, the shoulders, anywhere they could reach. The women began singing, and some started crying as they all remembered the horror of the day when twenty-seven people died in the explosion. An eighteen-year-old suicide bomber had gotten on the bus, yelled, "*Allah akhbar*," and pulled the trigger on his explosive belt. Rachel's two sons had died on that bus—two American boys who were on their way to volunteer for an Arab-Israeli peace camp for children.

An hour later, Julie and Rachel were driving back to Jerusalem.

Julie offered to stop so that they could get something to eat or drink, but Rachel said, "No, please take me to the Wall."

Julie said, "Isn't it enough for today?"

"No, I just want to sit there for awhile. You don't have to stay. Actually, I prefer to be alone right now. I will take a taxi back to my hotel."

They pulled up to the guarded entrance to the square in front of the Wailing Wall and said their good-byes, making plans to meet in two days.

"Thank you so much, Julie. I really needed your help today."

"I know. I am glad to help. I will see you later. *Shalom.*" Julie pulled away, looking back to see if she could see her friend's face. After going to the bus stop today, Rachel's eyes had a glazed, distant look that Julie had seen many times in people who had survived war zones. She knew it was the look of a person who was overwhelmed and traumatized. The remote stare meant they were split off from the present and haunted by their past. But Rachel had turned away from the car and was walking toward a line of people. At the gates were metal detectors, and Israeli security searched each person's bag.

Rachel politely greeted the security officers but fell silent as she numbly gazed out into the plaza, where hundreds of people faced a limestone wall that was as tall as ten men. She hardly heard the guard's English "thank-you" as she grabbed her purse and started to stumble down the slope to approach the wall. She stopped suddenly and looked up at the golden Dome of the Rock, the Muslim monument to Mohammed on the other side of the Wailing Wall. She felt the grip of anger, a stranglehold that blocked her breathing and made her mute.

Rachel felt flashes of hatred roar through her, like an angry animal seeking destruction. She imagined carrying a portable rocket-launcher on her shoulder, aiming it at the center of the pompous golden dome, and pulling the trigger. *I'd shoot it right at that golden dome and blow it sky-high!* she thought. She wanted to destroy something of the people who killed her two sons. *Boom!* she thought, imagining the explosion and seeing the flames and the pieces of the building flying everywhere. "One rock-and-mortar building for two living beings. Seems like a fair trade-off!" she muttered to herself.

"How could they kill randomly and without remorse? Where was their respect for life?" Rachel hissed under her breath. For a few minutes, she stood still and thought to herself. *God told us to turn the other cheek, but isn't it masochistic to keep getting hurt? Never again! I will not let anyone cause me such pain again! That crazy suicide bomber never knew about the years of suffering he caused me. Damn him to hell!*

Rachel held her chest to suppress the sobs that she felt rising. She thought, *If I had a shoulder rocket, I would stand here and aim it at the Temple Mount and then pull the trigger. Kaboom! No more golden dome glaring defiantly at me.*

She put her hand to her cheek and whispered, "God help me." She felt again the raging fury, a lust for blood and revenge that overwhelmed her when she stepped on the very ground, the very spot, of her sons' deaths—their homicides, their unjustified extinctions.

My joy, happy memories, love, and hope died on that day. The day my two sons were slaughtered! she thought, shuddering. That suicide bombing had happened only a few miles away from where she now stood, only a few years ago. *I used to live in a world of love, nurturing my children, watching them grow, learn, and explore the world. But the actions of one crazy man and one backpack of explosives forever changed the way I view the world. Now all I feel is deadness. Dead children and a dead heart.* She thought back to when she was raising her children, when she felt like she was part of the circle of life. *That was only some kind of New Age belief or Disney movie. Now I am only part of a circle of death.*

For a long time, Rachel stood in a one spot in the center of the large square. Her eyes were fixated on the lit golden dome peeking out over the Wailing Wall. Several security guards walked by her and slowly looked her up and down. She did not hear them whispering into their hand-held radios.

Suddenly, she heard a little boy's nearby scream, *"Ima!"* which meant Mamma in Hebrew. It snapped her back to reality. She watched as the boy ran into his mother's outstretched arms. Startled into action, Rachel walked to the women's side of the Wailing Wall and grabbed a white plastic chair. She pulled the chair to the very end of the women's section of the wall and tucked it into a tight corner. She took out a headscarf and wrapped it around her head securely and then pulled out some fabric to drape over her eyes for privacy. She wanted to shut herself off from the world, from questions, from looks. But as she glanced around, she saw that most of the women were deep into prayers or were gazing upward. Nobody noticed her. She started to cry again. She tried to suppress the deep, racking sobs, so that her body shook. She wanted to say something to God, but all she did was cry.

After a long time, maybe an hour or two later, she heard a little voice beside her. *"Shalom."* She turned to see a young girl, about four or five, dressed in Orthodox long sleeves and long skirts in plain, mute colors, wearing a black headscarf. The girl was holding out a rock to her. Rachel took it, saying the Hebrew word for thank you: *"Todah rabah."* The girl swirled around and ran back to her mother, who was surrounded by four more girls of varying heights, all of whom were praying. The girl grabbed her mother's skirt and then looked back at Rachel with her big brown eyes, full of sparkling wonder. The girl smiled sweetly and shyly and then turned her head into her mother's skirts.

Rachel looked at the rock. It was quite ordinary, a rock from a driveway or city sidewalk. But it was a gift from the heart. Rachel stopped crying and sat staring for several minutes at the rock. *Thank you, my little friend!* she thought. Eventually she looked up, straight up, and saw the unevenness of the Wailing Wall—how the limestone blocks did not make a smooth surface but jutted out. The uneven surface provided ledges for people to tuck their prayer notes in, for birds to nest in, and for greenery to grow.

Suddenly, Rachel realized that there was an analogy, a meaning, a symbol in the Wall. "In rocky times in life, new life can grow!" she exclaimed to herself. "Like the unexpected, selfless act of that sweet little girl. She is a stranger, yet she gave me her own treasured possession. An innocent act of love."

Rachel drew her breath in and held it. She suddenly tuned into the sounds around her: the whispered prayers, the movement of people, the hushed conversations, the scraping of chairs, the distant voices of security guards talking over the radio. She breathed deeply and looked up at the sky at the top of the Wall. The clouds were pink in the light of the setting sun. The Wailing Wall started to glow in a warm hue of golden light.

Rachel looked at the receding sun, the azure sky, the birds flying around the square of the Wailing Wall, the movements of people in prayer, and the jagged rocks of the Wall. She was here, she was present, she was aware. Tears came again to her eyes, but these tears were different. They were not tears of rage and blackness but tears of gentle sorrow and reluctant acceptance. *I don't know what is next, what's in my future. But I am ready to stop just barely surviving the day and to start enjoying colors again,* she thought wistfully.

chapter 13

KING SOLOMON WAS IN a bad mood. It was hot, the air was still, the sun scorching. It even penetrated the cloth cover that was his temporary work-station.

"Where is my food?" he growled, sitting at his table. The servant ran in with a plate and then tripped over the hem of his garment. The food scattered. He apologized to King Solomon, who was on the edge of explosion. "Get me more right now!" he bellowed.

"Master, let me pour you more wine," the shaken servant whispered.

King Solomon drank gulps of wine as the servant ran out of the tent to find a new plate of food. As he drank, he seethed with anger that was a thick as the day's heat. He wondered, *Why am I so irritable? What am I mad at? Why this fury?* He thought of no answer, and this made him anxious. He ordered more wine. *I am called the wisest man in the land, but I cannot answer my own questions! Why do I feel such hate at nobody in particular?* He felt like an animal that was trapped in a corner and ready to strike.

A new plate of food finally appeared, and Solomon attacked the plate with a singular focus. As he ate, the servant swept the spilled food off the floor and then quietly left the room. The only sounds that Solomon could hear were his own noises. The scraping of his plate, the chewing of his food, the smacking of his lips. A fly flew in and circled around his head and plate of food. His rage broke out, broiling like a fire consuming a lamb on a spit—crackling and sparking. He chased the fly around the tent and yelled, "Come here, you little donkey, and I will get you." Round and round he ran. He finally swatted the fly with his headscarf, and the tent was once again quiet.

King Solomon solemnly stared out of the tent, trying to understand his black anger. His week had gone well and the building plans were almost finished. The midday wine failed to calm him. He had no desire for a woman, which was highly unusual for him. *It might be dangerous for a woman if I was with her right now*, he thought.

He jumped up and paced around the tent, which was filled with shiny objects and soft pillows. Nothing was pleasing to him, and nothing could calm him. He was looking for another target.

Round and round he paced. Another servant came into the tent and announced that the building supervisors wanted to discuss some steps in building the temple. He angrily chased the servant out, yelling, "Don't bother me! Don't come in here again when you are not invited." Solomon sat for a few moments and then looked out of the tent. Across the plaza he saw a small group of rabbis talking, gesturing his way. They looked afraid—afraid of coming any closer and talking with him. Suddenly, they all bowed their heads and began to chant a prayer.

Solomon looked at them, wanting to yell at them and at their prayers. He fell to his knees and bowed his head. "What am I doing? God of my fathers, I am sorry. Please remove this anger from me! Help me! I am out of control!" He stayed facedown for a long time. Slowly stirring, he looked out of the tent and saw that the glowing evening light was falling on Jerusalem's walls. He stood and looked around. Everything looked so clear and bright to him, like he'd never noticed any of it before. He felt a sense of peace and walked out of the tent with a sense of mission.

Solomon ran to the tent containing the drawings of the temple and commenced working, redoing ideas and drawing new designs through the evening into morning. As the first streaks of morning sun stretched across the cloud-laden sky, Solomon told his assistant to go the women's quarters and bring him a woman who was already awake. He needed an alive and perky woman this morning, because he now had an abundance of healthy energy. *Why was I so angry yesterday? I don't want to be like my father—happy one moment and then suddenly sulking in his tent, singing songs to himself!* He laughed.

chapter 14

Moshe kept calling Sarah every five minutes. She would not answer her cell phone. He felt his stomach twinge and start cramping. He felt nauseous. An hour ago, there had been another suicide bombing. This bombing had been at Haifa University and killed seven students, injuring dozens of others. *What if she decided to visit her friends at Haifa University today? What if she was there? What if she's hurt?* he thought, holding his stomach as his ulcer painfully pulsed.

Everyone at his workplace had their radios on, listening to the news updates. Some people ran out of the room when they heard that someone they knew had been injured or killed. Moshe kept calling Sarah and getting her voice-mail. *I know we had an argument two nights ago, and so maybe she doesn't want to talk with me. But I need to talk with her .... just a few words! What if she's in the hospital? What if her family is hurt? I need to know if they all are okay!* he thought angrily, biting his fingernail.

Moshe finally told his boss that he had to go, and the boss waved with the back of his hand and said, "Go."

His irritation and his stomach pains grew as he drove from Ramat Gan to Tel Aviv. Even though he knew that the suicide bomb was in Haifa, not Tel Aviv, his anxiety was high.

Why doesn't she answer? Maybe she's hurt? Maybe she passed out? Maybe she had an accident, like cutting her hand instead of vegetables when she was listening to the news? Maybe she took a taxi to Haifa, in order to check on her parents? Maybe she is crying and needs me? he anxiously thought.

He finally pulled up to her white Bauhaus apartment and parked behind the row of cars in the parking area, blocking them in. He ran up three flights of stairs, holding his stomach, trying to catch his breath at the third flight, bending over and panting in front of her door. It took a moment, but he heard the distinct sounds of moaning, just like the noises Sarah makes during sex. He sharply breathed in and held his breath.

Then he heard it clearly. Sarah was groaning with a rumbling crescendo, followed by staccato yelps. A male voice then mimicked hers. Moshe realized at that moment that everything had changed.

chapter 15

RACHEL AND JULIE SAT outside at a coffee shop in the German Colony area of Jerusalem. The day was cloudless and warm, with few breezes. Rachel began telling Julie the story of her divorce after she discovered her husband had been having an affair for several years.

"Legally and ethically, he broke the social contract called marriage, so I had no problem with filing for a divorce. But the part that hurt me more was he didn't want me anymore. He wanted to be with someone else. So he made me feel like I was not good enough, pretty enough, sexy enough." Julie listened and nodded to what Rachel said.

"I didn't have to figure out a cost-benefit analysis of filing for a divorce. To me, my path was plain and simple. My trust was irrevocably broken, and I couldn't imagine ever trusting a man who had lied to me daily over the course of several years. Why would I want to be with such a man? How can you live with a liar?" Rachel asked Julie. Julie nodded and shrugged her shoulders.

Rachel continued, "To this day, I'll never understand why he did not have the courage to simply tell me that it was over and that he wanted to move on. I would've said, 'Okay, I love you but I let you go.' I wouldn't have been hysterical or bitter toward him. And he knew how I thought about relationships, that I believe that I cannot control him, or anyone else!" Julie looked at Rachel and touched her arm to comfort her.

"It's okay, Julie. I already knew it was over. I knew for awhile. When he was no longer excited to talk with me, to be with me, even to hold my hand, I knew that something had changed. And he was no longer interested in me sexually. I was just waiting for the end," Rachel winced and looked away sadly.

"I am sure that he loved you, at least for awhile," Julie said. "He used to tell me about you when he came to the refugee camps to help. I thought, I really thought, he was a good man," Julie said haltingly.

"Yes, there was a part of him that was good. But he ran away like a coward to the arms and legs of another woman. He never once said anything to me that even hinted that he might think that it was over, that things had changed between us. He voted with his feet and his sex organ."

Julie chuckled at Rachel's appropriation of the phrase "voting with your feet," which used to describe how political dissidents would flee communist countries. Julie added, "And many women vote with their mouths!" They both laughed.

Rachel continued. "But he didn't respect me enough to be honest with me! So why would I want to give him any more of me, no less the time of day!" She reflectively sipped her coffee and watched people walk by their table. "Adulterers don't want a divorce, because that's part of their game. They enjoy riding the waves of adventure upon women's backs. And it's funny how this new woman puts her trust in a man whom she knows is committing adultery. She naively expects him to marry her and be faithful to her!" she scoffed.

"Yes, I hear you. We all expect that we should be treated differently, that we are more deserving and special than others," Julie said. "I think that is why many people have trouble reaching out to others, helping the people I work with, the homeless and the displaced. I think it shakes their belief system—the belief that 'If I am a good and decent person, nothing tragic will happen to me.' Talking with good, kind people who survive tragedy pops their bubble of belief that they will be immune to the problems of disease, hunger, and disability," Julie said. Rachel nodded in agreement.

"So may I ask how the story ended between you and your husband?" Julie asked softly.

"Well," Rachel said, "one day, his lover sent me an e-mail and told me that she had been sleeping with him for several years, that he promised to marry her, and that she was pregnant. I packed his bags and changed the locks that day. When he came home late that evening, I confronted him and said something like, 'I now know that you have been with another woman for a long time. She told me. Any man who actually loved me would not do such a thing to me! So obviously you do not love me. Get out now!' I handed him his suitcases and plastic trash bags of books and papers. Of course, he tried to explain. 'But .... but ....' I told him, 'Good-bye. Just go!' I ushered him out of the door, locked it, and then slid down onto the floor and started crying. I hadn't shed a tear the whole day. I knew that, for me, it was over for good."

"I could hear him yelling outside the door. Yelling something about how he still loved me and that he was sorry. He kept knocking and then pounding on the door. When he realized the locks had been changed, he stood and yelled at the front door for about five minutes. I finally started laughing, laughing even more as he tried to find an excuse, saying it meant nothing, it was just sex, that he was a good person, and I was his soul mate. I surprised myself with how hard I was laughing. It's like I finally saw the whole charade, the acting that he had been doing, and how ridiculous all of it was."

"Then he yelled louder through the door that I couldn't divorce him because of our vows in front of God. He screamed, 'What about until death do us part? That means you must forgive me!' At that point, I opened a window and yelled back to him, and to the handful of neighbors who were looking out of their windows, 'If you are not acting godly, then our contract in front of God is null and void! A God-fearing man fears God enough not to lie to and cheat on his wife for *several years*! It's over! It's absolutely over with us! I will let my lawyer talk with you from this point on. I am done talking with you! Good-bye!' And that was basically the last time I spoke with him."

"That was the last time? Never again?" Julie asked incredulously.

"Yes. Of course, he tried to defend himself, and he bugged my lawyer endlessly. But in the end, when my lawyer read the e-mail that his lover sent to me, the divorce was no contest."

"Did those two marry?" Julie asked.

"I'm not sure. And I don't care. I realized recently that I had been living with a passive-aggressive man. He wanted to force me into divorcing him, so he'd look like the good guy, the one who was hurt. But it was really so he could do what he wanted, to be with the other woman, or maybe it was with *women* at that point. He just wanted me to leave him, so he could blame everything on me. Poor immature boy! He doesn't deserve to be married! Or maybe I should say it this way--another poor woman doesn't deserve to be treated the way he treated me!'" Rachel declared. Julie nodded in agreement.

Rachel paused to sip her coffee and then continued, "The thing I'll never understand is not why he left me, because things like that sometimes happen, but why he couldn't tell me that it was over. I think he felt powerful in his lying. It was a form of control over me. Plus he probably liked having sneaky sex. He was a bit perverted in some ways. I like honesty, so I'll never understand why he did not come clean and say what really was on his mind. That's partly why I'll never trust him anymore. He hides his real thoughts and disguises his actions. So how can I know what is real and what is a lie? Affair or no affair, I was living with a pseudo-man. How could I trust any single word that came out of his mouth in the future? I could already feel it was over. He felt so distant and alienated from me in the past few years. Near the end, it was very awkward between us, and he may have even abhorred me without me noticing. As King

Solomon wrote in Proverbs, 'Liars hate their victims.' I think he hated me in some ways." Rachel paused for a moment and then demonstratively stated, "And I don't want a hater and a liar as my intimate partner!"

chapter 16

KING SOLOMON FELT A soft hand on his shoulders and leaned back into the arms and fragrance of his current favorite wife. The pharaoh's daughter embraced him with her arms and legs. He reveled in the feeling of being held this way by a woman. Only a few women held him in such a manner, because most women were too afraid of him. They just received him and rarely responded to him sexually.

Solomon did not talk about his intimate desires with anyone, especially his women, because he knew that was not suitable for a king to do. His father had instructed him about these matters when he was an adolescent boy. Only this wife, the pharaoh's daughter, felt attuned to Solomon, anticipating what would please him and knowing how to respond to him. He did not have to say anything to her. She knew what to do and how to please him.

Solomon thought about the pharaoh's daughter and his attraction to her. He had negotiated with her father, the pharaoh of Egypt, to take her in marriage. And when she had entered Jerusalem in a huge caravan laden with gold and gifts, Solomon thought, *I did well to marry her.* Solomon built a special house for her so that she could live in conditions that suited her title as the pharaoh's daughter. He also let her build shrines to her sun gods and goddesses.

Solomon knew that wisdom was the study of differences,

but he did not understand why she was so different. Until the pharaoh's daughter, he thought that no woman saw his hidden vulnerable side, because each seemed to be frightened of him. But the pharaoh's daughter made *him* want to melt into her arms, to be cared for and encircled in love, not burdened with the suffering of others.

The pharaoh's daughter had confidently walked into his life. At first, her sexual knowledge astounded him. He responded to it. But in a matter of months, Solomon began to dislike and even hate her for her sexual acuity. In Solomon's mind, a wife of his should not be so assertive and sexually knowledgeable, because that meant she had had a lot of experience in other beds. He did not want a "pre-owned" woman and had instructed his advisors never to send a divorced woman into his chambers. He wanted them fresh and sweet as lilies.

One day King Solomon got an urge to visit the pharaoh's daughter. He ordered a horse and galloped to her house. When the pharaoh's daughter saw him that evening, she bowed deeply before him. Her long, shiny black hair fell down around her when she bowed. She stood up and smiled confidently, staring directly in his eyes.

They walked together and kneeled before statues of Molech and Ashtoret. Musicians made a rhythmic melody, and young girls with flowers in their hands circled the altar. Incense filled the room with a sweet haze. Solomon glanced at the pharaoh's daughter and was aroused by seeing her bow before the altars. He flashed on their private moments when she bent at such an angle for his pleasure. His eyes glazed over, and buzzing started in his ears. He signaled her to follow him. *What beauty! What power!* he thought as she walked behind him into the bedchamber.

chapter 17

AFTER HIDING IN HIS apartment for three days and crying until he was dehydrated and thirsty, Moshe finally opened his shades and looked out onto the city street. He plugged his phone in to charge and saw that there were a dozen messages for him. Some were from work, most were from friends. He called up his closest friend, Golan, who had called him at least five times. They had gone through school and then the army together, so they knew when something was not quite right with each other.

Golan said, "When you didn't answer after the fifth call, I ran over and opened your apartment door. I checked your pulse and then left so you could sleep. I heard through the grapevine that your engagement with Sarah was off. So I called your boss to let him know that you would be gone for a few days."

"Thank you, my friend. Let's get a coffee. I have a splitting headache and cannot think straight," Moshe said. Half an hour later, they were eating a big breakfast at a café on HaShalom Street.

Golan said, "Okay let's hear it. What happened?"

Moshe described the events of the day he went to her apartment. "When I unlocked her apartment door and saw Sarah with another man doing the Garden of Eden dance, I just looked at her silently. Then I walked out of the apartment and wandered around the streets of Tel Aviv for hours, not caring whether I got lost, which I did. It wasn't because our brilliant Tel Aviv officials rename the streets after their favorite heroes every few blocks, but because I was too confused, trying to process what I had just seen. It was only when I returned to my apartment that the floodwaters starting pouring out of me—endless streams of tears, profanity, disgust, and anger. I opened the vodka that I had purchased on my way home, knowing that I would need some heavy sedating that night. I woke up two days later with a pounding headache and empty bottle." Moshe stuffed bites of omelet and potatoes in his mouth and took a long drink of coffee. "They say women love and men think. But I say, if women can think, then men can love. And I loved her—furiously," Moshe explained angrily.

"You have a good heart, Moshe! Most men would've found a replacement very quickly," Golan said with a smile.

"Thanks for checking on me, man. You've been a good friend!" Moshe said to Golan.

Moshe and Golan talked for another hour, and then Golan said that he had to get back to work. They promised to meet again for Shabbat dinner. Moshe wandered around the Dizengoff shopping center for a few hours and went to the food store on the bottom floor. There he bought some bagels, cheese, olives, hummus, and more vodka. He went home, turned on the TV, and drank until the bottle was empty.

Like any good friend, Golan told all of Moshe's friends what had happened. They started calling each other after Moshe did not return any of their phone calls, texts, or e-mails. Then a group of his army buddies arrived at Moshe's door, pounding until he let them in. Moshe knew that they would break down his door and/or smash in through the windows if he did not respond.

His buddies immediately swarmed into his apartment. Like a well-trained military unit, each took on a different task without talking. One opened the blinds and windows. Another picked up trash. The third called his family. A fourth made him coffee.

And the fifth sat beside him and wiped Moshe's face with a cold, wet towel.

They all convened at the small kitchen table and started asking about what had happened.

"What did she do to you?"

"Did you see this coming?"

"What did you tell her?"

"What are you going to do?"

These men knew how to get information, not only because of interrogation techniques that they had learned together in the army, but because they had shared so many intimate details with each other during the long hours of patrol on the Lebanese border or when they were stationed near the Gaza strip with terrorists shooting poorly made missiles at them.

This group was bonded in the deepest sense of friendship. They had fought for a common goal, literally protected each others' backs, and spent all their waking hours together, whether training, entertaining, or even restraining each other in practice fighting. They knew how to gauge when testosterone was heating up emotions, overwhelming rationality. But at this moment, the psychologist of the group, Edgar, had to remind them, "Hey, hey! Back off! This is humiliating for Moshe." They backed off with their questions and started talking about sports.

Moshe's friends sat around his apartment and consoled him all day, forcing him to eat food and drink water, talking about all possible topics—soccer, sex, politics, women. Finally they talked about Sarah. Edgar, a Russian immigrant labeled a lone wolf in the military because he had no family to go home to during the Sabbath, was the leader of the pack in terms of psychological insight.

Edgar said to Moshe, "Who was rejecting whom here? Is Sarah rejecting you by sleeping with some scruff off the street? Or are you rejecting her when she begs you to forgive her because she is not trustworthy and good enough for you?" Edgar kept driving this point home to Moshe. He pressed the matter even further:

"Maybe she is emotionally turning away from you because you, on some level, were rejecting her? How about those times that you would look at women's breasts and asses as they walked by, while you sat in a café with Sarah?"

Moshe stared at Edgar, half with anger and half with surprise. "I rejected her? Who proposed marriage to her and bought her a ring? Sarah rejected me!"

Edgar knew the secret of psychological catharsis—the purging of emotions that otherwise would fester in one's mind and burn a wound more painful than a cigarette butt on exposed flesh. Edgar took Moshe one more step. "Maybe you actually hated her and kept having sex with her to prove your manhood to yourself and to your mother?"

"No, no, no! I loved her like no other!" Moshe screamed. He started crying in front of his friends.

Many believed that a man crying in front of other men meant the end of the line—the end of the ability to disguise and suppress one's emotions, of bravery, and of strength. But Edgar, a clever psychologist, knew that this was the end of Moshe's false bravado, the end of his denying the hurt and pain that was evident on his face. Men in the Israeli army, like all armies on the planet, were trained to control and suppress all emotional reactions so they could function in the military. But Edgar knew the difference— this was no longer an army environment. This was life. Edgar's operating principle was that healthy emotions make an Israeli man a good lover and a good father.

A few of Moshe's army friends shifted their eyes and bodies uncomfortably at the moment of Moshe's emotional explosion, but Edgar embraced Moshe and said comforting words to him. Then the other men in the apartment joined him. They locked their arms in a tight circle around Moshe and Edgar and began to sing the Israeli national anthem and other feisty army songs. That gradually quieted Moshe's sobs.

chapter 18

RACHEL SAT IN A coffee shop at Tel Aviv University with her American friend Catherine. Catherine was a red-headed beauty with intense blue eyes and a confident air. Catherine was currently enrolled in an Ulpan Hebrew language course at the university. When she finished, she planned to take courses on psychotherapy and feminism during the academic year.

They talked about their lives. Rachel had three children with her former husband; Catherine had no children from her four marriages. Rachel cupped her chin in her hands and leaned forward, saying, "I remember the sweet years of my kids' early childhood, when they were so innocent, trusting, curious, and loving. I would hug and kiss them all the time and tousle their hair. I especially loved the first year of life. I loved their snuggling close to me for warmth, love, and protection, their hungry little stomachs, their curious little minds, their pudgy little bodies that grew rapidly every day. It was so very amazing. I never felt so wanted and necessary to someone's existence!"

Catherine nodded in response and quietly sipped her cappuccino.

Rachel sighed and said, "I was so amazed at this cute little being with miniature fingers and tiny limbs. I would watch every little breath and earnestly pray to God that their breathing would continue. I was so scared that something would happen to this fragile being and it would be my fault. And their little smiles just melted my heart. I will never forget it!"

Rachel paused, wiped the corners of her eyes, cleared her throat, and then continued speaking. "I loved those early years of parenting, even though I was physically exhausted all the time. It was amazing to watch a little one grow rapidly and then start crawling, standing, babbling, pointing, running away from me, and then running back to cling to me so I could feel their little hearts beat fast. That was the ultimate thrill to me."

"Even more than sex?" Catherine asked. They both laughed.

"Except that." Rachel looked down at her coffee and said, "But now, now what do I have? All that care and work, all the attention, cooking, cleaning, washing, loving, protecting ... now I have nothing. A husband who thought his coworker was more attractive than his wedding vows. Two dead sons. And a daughter who will hardly speak to me on the phone and has tattoos, piercings, a live-in lover. All of my emotional, financial, psychological, and social investment was in my family. And then it all disappeared!" Rachel frowned. "My emotional bank account in my children and husband is decimated. I hoped to have a little bit of payback, or at least gratitude, from all my years of caring and giving."

Rachel looked at her poised, regal friend and told her, "I feel like Mount St. Helens in Washington state when it blew its stack. Lava rolled down its hills, knocking over huge pine trees and frying all the greenery and undergrowth. My life exploded. Everything was flattened, going up in smoke so quickly."

"Did you see it coming?" Catherine asked softly.

"I could feel that my marriage was splitting apart, that there was nothing that I could do about it. He no longer looked at me with love and enthusiasm but with a kind of shiftiness and unease. He avoided eye contact with me. I knew—oh, I knew. I'd felt it was over between us even before I learned of his affair. Then I found out that he was having sex with another woman. In the very first moment that I saw him after my discovery, I said to him firmly and quietly, 'If you want to be with another woman, then get out—get out of my life!' I could say that because I had already prepared myself for that moment. I had rehearsed it all in my head because I knew that it was coming soon. I became aware of a great gulf and awkwardness between us before I knew about the affair. He no longer held my hand or lovingly held me after sex. Our sex had become goal orientated—but only toward *his* goal." Catherine rolled her eyes, and they both laughed.

"But once I confronted him, he tried to coax me back, telling me that I was his 'soul mate' and that God wanted us to be together. That made me mad. He wanted to maintain appearances of a marriage after I found out about his affair. Why pretend to be what it wasn't?" Catherine nodded fiercely in agreement.

"He kept insisting that I forgive him, instead of taking responsibility for what he had done to me. It was like he wanted to stay in his horizontal thinking and never go vertical. He broke his promise to me, so I felt no obligation to try to conduct a unilateral repair on a broken system. He showed me what he wanted—he wanted another woman, not me. So I gave him what he wanted, even though he said that it wasn't what he wanted. 'What the hell do you want?' I asked him. Of course, he couldn't say what he wanted. But his actions spoke quite clearly. And I was done, so done, with him. I wasn't going to enable his deceit by trying to reconcile with him and be his sex toy. I'll use them, but I don't want to be one!"

Catherine burst out laughing at that comment and then covered her mouth, "Oh, I'm sorry."

"No," Rachel said. "It is funny, though so ironic," she said, smiling faintly. "No wonder so many of my clients are depressed. It's hard to feel continuously connected to someone. Even with a lover, you get brief moments of ecstatic closeness, and then you fall away from each other in bed. And then maybe fall away for good. And you have those inevitable misunderstandings, miscommunications, and frustrations with each other. Then, if you are fortunate, you claw away at the wall, the separation, to get the closeness back."

Catherine nodded. Then her cell phone rang. She grabbed her purse, pulled it out, and answered it quickly. Rachel gestured in the direction of the restroom and left the table. She did not want to tell Catherine how depressed she had felt recently. She knew that her friend would suggest therapy. Rachel thought, *I know what the problem is and what I need.*

Rachel thought about the events in the past few years with her former husband and knew she would like to start dating a really nice guy. *But I don't want to be sexually close to someone I don't love and trust. I know from my therapy practice that many people use sex to be close to someone, and after sex, they will decide whether or not they will like and trust the person.* She washed her hands in the warm water, watching the water cascade gently over her hands. *Have sex first and ask questions later. How very stupid and dangerous!* she thought as she firmly turned off the faucet.

As Rachel walked back to her seat in the coffee shop, she thought, *Yeah, but look at me. I'm infatuated with a married man!* She suddenly realized that Mr. Hit-and-Run was very similar to her father. *So maybe that explains my unfulfilled longing for an unavailable man like Mr. Hit-and-Run? My father was so busy with his career and then the upkeep of the yard and house on the weekends that he hardly spent any time with me when I was growing up. But my father isn't such a stranger, because he isn't that complicated to understand. He likes his meals on time, his clothes cleaned, his television and newspaper after dinner with no interruptions. At meals, he only wants to talk about his day and office politics or what yard work he accomplished.* Rachel looked over to see that Catherine was still talking on her cell phone. She stopped at an empty table and pulled out a piece of paper. She quickly wrote a poem.

I'm missing you,
Father,

wanting whom you
could have been
wishing what you
could have given
me, Dad,
some comfort and
soothing and
words of wisdom
when
I needed them.
I'm missing what
could have been
when
I was a child and
needed a friend.
You missed me in a
different way back then.

chapter 19

KING SOLOMON LUXURIATED IN his quarters, looking at the sketches of the temple drawn on papyrus. Solomon requested specific designs, based on what he thought would be pleasing to God. The dry heat of the summer day hung like a heavy tree branch about to break. He threw down the drawings and sprang to his feet. He was restless and hot. He roamed his chambers like a tiger. The palace guards saluted him each time he made a lap around the chambers. He mumbled to them, "Please no more," with growing irritation.

He finally stopped circling and angrily ordered the only salve that he knew to comfort him: a woman. The guards ushered in a woman who appeared to be the age of his first daughter. He stopped in his tracks and said loudly, "Not her, she is too young." His advisor Ahishar, the manager of his palace, whispered to him that she was of age. Solomon nodded in response and then dismissed everyone with the flick of a hand.

Sure enough, once the room was vacated, Solomon unveiled her to see a young face. But she had sorrowful and angry eyes. She bowed before him. When he lifted up her head with one hand, he saw that she was crying. He called for his advisor to return and remove her from his chambers. "Bring me another," he commanded.

His advisor came back, smiling sharply, with a saucy woman

who talked and laughed loudly. Every time she had previously visited his chambers, Solomon had enjoyed her company. "My king, I am here to serve you," she declared, looking at him in a sexually suggestive way and turning her butt to the side while she bowed deeply. Solomon laughed and sent his men away.

After some time of intimacy, relaxation, and sleep, Solomon arose peacefully and returned to work on the temple plans. An image of the crying girl he sent away from his chambers last night kept returning to his mind. He knew that she would be safe in the women's quarters. She would be adopted as family and taken care of for the rest of her life, now that she had been touched, even once, by Solomon. But he never learned her name, and the details of her face were hazy. He probably would never see her again, because he had signaled to his advisor Ahishar that she should not be brought back to his chambers. He wondered what had made her cry.

He told his advisors to find out why the girl had cried before him. They ran back to the women's quarters and then dashed back to Solomon's quarters. "She is terrified of you. She thinks she has no other choice after both of her parents died in a battle of clans in the Judean desert. So she has no dowry. And she is deeply infatuated with a man with arms of steel and eyes like swords, who fights valiantly," they reported.

"Find and bring me this man," Solomon commanded.

Soon, the guards brought Enoch into Solomon's chambers. "Tell me your story," Solomon abruptly said to the man.

Enoch started telling Solomon where he was born, how he was raised, where he fought, and what his allegiances were. Solomon asked, "And whom do you love?"

Enoch laughed loudly and said, "Only one! She was only eleven years old when I met her, and she is still full of innocent joy and curiosity."

"Tell me the story," King Solomon demanded.

Enoch was surprised at such a request from the king, but he started telling the story of how he was coming home from a very important win on the battlefield. It was a *hamseen* day, a suffocatingly hot desert phenomenon. He had trotted up to a small village on his camel wearing an embroidered cape, a flashing sword strapped to his waist. Many women were standing around a well, waiting their turn to get water. They started talking, yelling, and trying to get his attention—he was handsome and obviously came from a wealthy family. A young girl had stood near the side of the well and shyly offered him water from her cup, her head bowed and the cup lifted high over her head. "She was the only one who offered me water," Enoch said to King Solomon.

Enoch told him how he'd stepped off his camel and walked toward her, pushing the women aside, scattering and silencing them with the sweep of his arms. He was only an adolescent himself, but he towered over her little frame. Taking the cup slowly from her, he said, "Girl, what is your name? Who is your father?" She slid her empty hands down from the top of her head to cover her whole face and did not respond to him.

He asked his questions again, more softly this time, and leaned close to her face. She peeped out between her fingers, still holding them to cover most of her face. "Ruth, sir. My father is Benjamin, of the tribe of Judah." Seeing him right in front of her face, she grinned. Her smile spread out beyond the palms covering her face, and her eyes, peeking out between her fingers, twinkled. Enoch smiled back, connecting silently with her gentle eyes. "At that moment, I knew that she was the one that I wanted as my wife," he said to King Solomon.

Enoch described how he then turned away, pushed through the murmuring women, mounted his camel, and glanced back one more time at Ruth. The women knew what his look meant, but Ruth just blushed from the attention and started running away from the well.

Solomon fell silent when he heard the story. He thought about how his father, King David, had sent Bathsheba's husband to the dangerous front line of a battle so that he could have Bathsheba.

Solomon did not want to repeat that offense. He nodded to Enoch and then whispered to his advisor, who ran out immediately. He whispered to one of his guards, and the guard ran out. Solomon gestured to Enoch and said, "Please sit for a moment. Eat and drink. I am told about your valor on the battlefield. You have served me well."

Soon the guard ran back and handed Solomon a bag, which Solomon placed beside him. Within ten minutes, his advisor returned with a veiled woman, but they stayed in the back of the room. Solomon told Enoch, "Come forward to me." Enoch walked near Solomon and bowed deeply. Solomon stood up and placed a small, heavy bag in Enoch's hand. Everyone in the room could hear the clink of coins. "For you, my loyal servant." And then he gestured for his advisor to come forward with the woman. Solomon indicated that his advisor should remove her veil. The woman kept her chin tucked down and her eyes lowered. Enoch looked at the woman and then gasped. "Ruth!"

Hearing her name, Ruth looked up with surprise and whispered, "Enoch!" King Solomon pulled Enoch and Ruth's hands together and said, "Let you two marry. I give you my blessings." Everyone in King Solomon's quarters smiled and cheered. "Praise to our King Solomon!" they yelled.

chapter 20

Six weeks after Moshe had encountered Sarah in intimacies with another man and left her with her mouth and legs open, he met her again.

"How are you, Moshe?" Sarah asked, a slight look of guilt on her face.

"Fine. *Shalom*." Moshe began briskly walking away from her.

"Moshe, stop. Please stop!"

"Oh, now you want to say that to me! You should've said that to *him* so you wouldn't have to say it to me," he snarled.

"Moshe, don't. I love you. Don't you still want to marry me?" she pleaded.

"In fact, no. And no again. I've found someone else!" he declared with a vengeful sneer.

"Then you must take back your cheap ring so you can give it to her. I did not like it anyway!" Sarah curtly replied, throwing the ring precariously close to a gutter in the street. It bounced off his shoe. She pivoted and wobbled briefly on her gold four-inch heels and then walked away. She leaned into a shop window to check her hair. Moshe thought he saw her looking back at him in the reflection.

She'll never know the truth, Moshe thought. He had not found a new girlfriend. He had found a sexual outlet among the prostitutes. He knew where to go to access them, having learned as an adolescent where "those" houses were and how to gain entrance without neighbors seeing him go in.

But this time, Moshe was so angry at Sarah that he sought some new brothels—ones with Arabic prostitutes. For some reason, Sarah's betrayal made him unable to have sex with Jewish prostitutes. He discovered that his impotence was not a problem when he went to Arabic prostitutes.

Moshe enjoyed the experience more with Arabic than Jewish prostitutes. Despite the vacant look in most of the prostitutes' eyes and the mechanical ways by which they accomplished their work, Moshe found that the Arabic prostitutes were much more submissive than the Jewish prostitutes. Jewish prostitutes seemed to have a defiant attitude toward him, no matter how much he paid for sex. Moshe thought that maybe many of those Jewish prostitutes were working to earn money for expensive purses, shoes, and clothing, which he saw strewn about in the corners of their shabby rooms. But the Arabic prostitutes seemed to passively tolerate his male machinations and eagerly grabbed the money once it ended, as if their survival depended on it. These women looked sad and angry, not defiant.

The last time he visited a brothel was several years ago. Since that time, Moshe's political views about Israeli-Arab politics had shifted more toward enforcing security than advocating for peace. So he found a perverse delight in patronizing an Arabic brothel. Moshe justified his Arabic brothel visits by smirking to himself, *I'm contributing to the economy of the West Bank, which I hear is an area of high unemployment.*

chapter 21

FATIMA WAS A YOUNG Israeli-Arab woman with shiny, long, dark hair and warm brown eyes. Several years ago, she'd made the decision to wear a hijab and to be a practicing Muslim. She lived with her family in the same small stone house in southeast Jerusalem where her ancestors had lived for several centuries. Over the past decade, their neighborhood had become more and more Jewish, making them more and more uncomfortable. Many times her family had seriously discussed moving three miles east to an Arab village near Mount Scopus, in order to feel safer and live more freely. But they always decided, "This is our fathers' land and house, and we will not move."

Fatima's forty-five-year old mother Najib was obese, with a creased face showing a web of many lines, like a fractured windshield. She used to describe her aged face, with some degree of pride, as the "battle scars from raising nine children."

Fatima and her younger siblings commuted every day on city buses to reach their Muslim school. They were the same public buses that Jews took, the same buses that were blown up almost weekly.

During the two Intifadas, Najib had been in near hysterics every day. When they returned from school, she squeezed them tightly in her arms, saying prayers to Allah in Arabic, practically suffocating them in her robes until they finally complained loudly. "Mom, enough!"

Breaking away from their mother's embrace made Najib cry. Then it took another thirty minutes for the children to console their mother and sufficiently convince her that they were safe, alive, and ready to play with their friends. They ran out of the apartment without eating a snack, in fear that their mother would once again break into tears and need more consolation. When darkness fell, they returned home for a hot meal to face their teary-eyed mother. They awkwardly sat together and quickly ate the warm pita with a sauce of hot tomatoes and lentils with spices, and sometimes a piece of fruit. Then the children ran to various corners of the small home to work on their homework.

The morning hours came too quickly. At six o'clock, Fatima's mother Najib put on the coffee for her husband and began scolding the children to wash and dress. By six forty-five, they were on a city bus to cross Jerusalem, which was sometimes so snarled in traffic that they missed their first class. On the bus, Fatima tried to surround herself with her younger sisters, because at age sixteen, she already was aware of men's stares, Jewish and Arab men alike. Even without makeup, even under a modest hijab, she felt their intense, fixed gazes.

Maybe it was her eyes that attracted them. She had a gentle but curious gaze. And she was not afraid of looking at men directly. This was part of her growing rebellion toward her strict family life, which constantly felt like a noose tightening around her neck. She did not mind wearing modest clothes, which provided her a kind of shelter from which she could observe and explore the world. She thought men's steady gazes and glowing eyes were quite interesting. She stared back, but then she felt awkward, giggled, and turned quickly away. She would slyly look back to see if the men were still staring at her. They were, often with a slight smile on their lips. This made her a little anxious but at the same time more curious.

What're they smiling about? she thought. She knew her own

body very well, having explored its surfaces and pleasure points in the privacy of the night. But she did not quite understand the message that the men on the city buses were sending and why she felt her skin prickle when she saw those stares.

Fatima especially liked to look at the suntanned, muscle-bound Israeli soldiers that crowded the bus in the morning. They typically stood in the center of the bus, intentionally not sitting, holding the bus strap above their heads and gripping their machine guns with their other hand. They seemed so solid, alert, and yet very calm compared to the Arabs who often sported anxious, angry, or frowning faces. The soldiers talked quietly to each other or on their cell phones. *So in control,* thought Fatima, *unlike my father.*

Fatima's father worked two jobs—construction and olive-picking. He often came home several hours later than the children returning from play. He was too tired to do more than kiss each child on the head, kiss his wife Najib on the cheek, wash his hands and face, and then sit down to watch television. Najib brought food to him to eat there, because everyone else had already eaten. He sat there, yelling at everyone from his chair and demanding that the children leave him alone. After chasing the children to bed, Najib tried to tell him about the day's events, but he continued slowly chewing on pita bread, or sucking on olives, watching the Al Jazeera network. Najib's news did not compare to the world news, so he just ignored her.

Fatima did not say much to her mother anymore. She felt awkward around her mother, and slightly embarrassed by her. She did not want to tell Najib that she did not want a wedding ceremony if she ever married. She knew that would shock her mother badly. She decided to express her real opinions by writing in a diary. She opened the lavender pages and wrote, *Dear Diary, You are*

the only one who will know my truth, my innermost thoughts. Fatima.

Fatima must have attended more than two hundred weddings in her young life. Each was an extravagant, fluffy event. Women got very excited for weeks, if not months, in their preparations for festivities, parties, and gift-giving. Fatima did not want that kind of attention paid to her. *If I marry,* she wrote in her diary, *I want to say my vows without the term forever, so as not to presuppose anything. I just want to say my wedding vows with my husband, so I can have sex without guilt. Say the marriage vows and then have sex. No big celebration. The rest will be waiting and seeing how things turn out. No promises of forever. That's what I want. What good are those promises if you can hardly get along day to day at home?*

In Fatima's community, women talked about their weddings as the biggest day in their lives. This made Fatima angry and nauseous. *Is that all to expect out of life?* she thought to herself. Already, half of the girls in her class were engaged to be married. Most of them planned to marry next year, once they finished their courses. All those girls wanted to talk about was their upcoming weddings. Fatima thought they were snooty and arrogant.

At school, Fatima flew under the gossip radar, because she was a good student and did not have a boyfriend. The girls in her class did not find her interesting because she did not provide them with juicy tidbits about anyone. "Ah, who will marry whom? How boring! Tell me when it is over!" Fatima declared, to the surprise and anger of her classmates and sisters.

They think that they are so special, she wrote in her diary. *But I think that my school-mates are marrying for personal salvation from their pain, loneliness, and lack of meaning. And they will avoid the social ridicule of not being married by a certain age. I know that women feel very special and chosen when they marry. But they take it to the extreme. They think that they have a unique love that is different than all other humans!*

But I don't want to be locked in by marriage. I want to be free! Free to explore, learn, grow, change, travel, experiment, and succeed in life without being obligated to the commands of my family! I want to know that I alone obtained what I get in life. That is power! I will do it, even if everyone tells me don't go, don't change, don't try …just get married and have kids. Diary, you are my witness. I want out of here! she wrote in big letters. Then she closed her diary and hid it behind the books stacked in the corner of her room.

chapter 22

SOLOMON FOLLOWED A NIGHTLY ritual after dinner. He withdrew to his chambers, bathed, sat quietly, and read documents. His advisors, including Behnaiah and Azariah, interrupted him at this hour only if there were military-related matters to discuss. Solomon liked to read the ancient sages. He found their wisdom profound and useful. He also utilized the sages' knowledge when he met with people in his court during the day.

As a king, Solomon knew he was admired, honored, revered, and even worshipped. But he also knew he always had to walk and speak carefully, knowing that people expected and needed him to speak with godly wisdom. He liked the challenge of understanding different points of view and the strengths and weaknesses of various approaches. Some days he trembled in his room before entering the court. He felt the weight of making decisions that affected people and that others did not want to make.

Solomon also saw much sorrow in his court. It emanated from the eyes of the people—a paradox of expressions, exuding despair but seeking hope. They were his people. He wanted to help them, to reach out to them, and to relieve their suffering. Sometimes he succeeded, but other times his words triggered torrents of tears and wailing.

The one issue that the sages did not provide much guidance

on was sexuality. The sages had plenty to say about marriage and rules about entering and exiting it. Solomon did not have anyone he could talk with regarding his issues with women. As king, he did not want to reveal his private side to his friends or advisors. And he never found a woman who he wanted to talk with about anything for more than a few minutes. They all seemed easy enough to read. They wanted security. They wanted babies. They were predictable.

But lately, the queen of Sheba had been speaking to Solomon through messengers. He was intrigued by the communication. *Could these really be her words?* he thought. For years, he had longed for a woman who understood the deeper side of him, the part that he protected and disguised. *I must meet this queen, Solomon decided.*

After finishing his nightly reading, Solomon signaled to his personal servant that he wanted a woman in his bed. Tonight, his advisor brought a beautiful adolescent girl to his chambers. He had sent her away many times before because she was too young and too afraid of his advances. Now she looked and walked differently. She knew what to do when Solomon received her in his private chambers.

The women must have taught her some things about life, he thought. She walked softly up to him but kept her eyes averted. He lifted her downcast face gently by her chin. Her eyes sparkled, but her face showed tension, and she trembled. He wrapped his arms around her, and she hugged him tightly.

In the morning, he left her sleeping in his royal bed. He felt joyful and exuberant, running down the dusty road to where they were building the temple. *Maybe I should marry this one?* he thought.

Solomon brought together his entire household to celebrate the Passover meal, which that year totaled more than two hundred women, one hundred seventy-eight children, eighty-three servants, sixteen palace guards, and all of his advisors. The evening was festive, full of singing, talking, and laughing.

Solomon gathered all of his children together and told them stories about the sacrifices and triumphs of his father, King David, and of Abraham, Moses, and other forefathers of Israel. His eyes were shining as the children looked at him with awe. Only little Ayala, his favorite child, stood up and asked to speak. She shyly asked Solomon, "What about God?"

The topic on everyone's tongue was the possible visit of the famed queen of Sheba. Messengers on camels had traveled weeks to exchange invitations, but King Solomon wanted her to wait until the temple was complete.

King Solomon's enthusiasm over the topic of the queen of Sheba made the women laugh out loud, but each of them secretly felt jealous over his excitement about the queen's replies to Solomon's messages. Many women in Solomon's household wanted to be the number-one woman, the head of house, and the queen of the land. It was the ultimate prize.

Solomon's restless energy had touched them all. And he kept adding new women to the women's quarters. King Solomon had vast resources of wealth to expend on his intimate adventures, but he was not satisfied with any of the women, and none of the women were satisfied with their status with him. Each of them wanted to have his heart, to be the central focus of his attention and his ardor. But now his concentration was focused on building a temple to honor God.

Solomon was never satisfied. Women throughout the land talked among themselves about that, not understanding why. The ones who wanted to try to become his queen studied how to dance, play music, and sing. And the smart ones studied more private skills, like bedroom proficiency, with the goal of pleasing him.

But Solomon did not keep a woman very long before returning her to the women's quarters. They never understood why, and he never gave them a reason. Solomon would one day just decide that it was enough and gently escort the woman to his door, handing her over to his advisor, who would accompany the woman on her walk to the women's quarters. Everyone knew that this meant it was over for her.

Solomon's endings of his interactions with women happened without a noticeable pattern. Some women lasted weeks, some months, and others just days. Of course, when the rejected woman arrived in the women's quarters, they peppered her with questions and then threw salt in her emotional wounds by gossiping about her.

The few women who stayed longer with Solomon had the greater status in the women's quarters. One woman, the pharaoh's daughter, had lasted two years in King Solomon's bed. She had her own room in Solomon's quarters during that period of time. Then Solomon built a special house just for her. The women disliked her, not only because of her striking beauty, but because she did not tell her secrets to them. So they shunned her. Before her house was built, she stood separately from the other women, quietly tending to her child.

There was a stigma for being a wife of Solomon, because some people in Jerusalem viewed them as prostitutes for the king. Solomon's concubines were not given wife status. Some women called that group the "leftovers." Some did not want to be his wife. By not taking the title of wife, the women signaled to King Solomon that they were independent and strong, which were qualities that they knew excited him. They might occasionally find their way back into his bed if they flirted enough with him during the large family gatherings. King Solomon enjoyed the attention of these women to a certain extent. His male pride was stroked when the women chased him. But he discovered that their personalities were filled with jealousy and haughtiness, qualities he did not like. So he ended up sending them away within days of their triumphant return to his private quarters. They did not realize that he could hardly tolerate being around them once the dance of intimacy ended.

The upcoming visit of the queen of Sheba was not only Solomon's focus but also the talk of his whole household and many priests in the community. Many were shocked that he was interested in a woman who worshipped foreign gods. "How can he pursue her? This is forbidden!" they whispered.

The priests furtively talked among themselves about King Solomon. They worried that if he got intimately involved with such a woman, he might start worshipping her gods. There would be serious consequences if the king of Israel did that. It would break one of God's commandments given to Moses and the tribe of Israel.

The priest Zabud, who was Solomon's close friend, spoke to Solomon one day when he entered the nearly completed temple. Zabud said, "Do not continue with her. You might break the first of Moses' commandments: you shall have no other gods before me. Listen to the wisdom of your people. The laws of Judaism forbid kings to marry foreign women. You must stop this!"

Solomon said to Zabud, "You are like a brother to me. But leave me alone! I won't marry her." Solomon walked out of the unfinished temple into the blinding sun.

Solomon was intrigued by the queen of Sheba, not only because she was a woman in charge of a country but because their occasional communications were full of riddles and mysteries. Solomon was told by many messengers that while queen was not the most physically beautiful woman in the region, she had a sparkle and a wit that immensely entertained her court and her visitors. He wanted to see her in person. He also wanted to meet a woman who was curious about the world, and who was not just focused on how to get him to marry her.

chapter 23

GALIT WAS A MODERN Israeli woman long blonde hair, blue eyes, and a big sexual appetite. She started having sex at age fifteen and living with a man at age sixteen. Her favorite clothing was tight black spandex that showed her cleavage. Galit was a "doer," never slowing down in talking, walking, or thinking until time to sleep. Her life included several parties and dinners out with friends every week.

Galit liked men of all shapes and sizes. She admired men's tight muscles and sleek abdomens. She worked every day to maintain her petite figure. Galit was a gym fanatic who ran her curves off her body. She spent hours a day lifting weights to sculpt her arms, like a man. She went on a daily search for any suggestion of fat on her body. When she went to the Tel Aviv bars at night with her friends, she wore low-cut, sleeveless dresses that tightly clung to her gym-firm buttocks. She didn't care which of her friends went along, as long as there were men at the bar. What she really liked, craved, desired, and yearned for was male attention.

Galit liked to play with men on several levels. And she really liked it when they gave her stuff. She asked and they gave. To Galit, men were her little slot machines—give them a tug in the right places and she would be rewarded. If not, then she, without begging or tears, simply went to a different slot machine and tried pulling his levers. "This is what blond hair and zero body fat gets you in the land of men," she proclaimed to her friends.

Galit preferred to hang out with men rather than women because she liked their protectiveness, thinly disguised sexual attraction, and desire for her attention. Most of all, she liked free stuff. She liked when they bought her things and paid her bills at the food store, at restaurants, and movies. She also liked a male audience when she criticized other women. She eliminated some of the competition that way and made her male friends gravitate toward her superiority.

Being one of the tribe of toned, skinny women with blond hair, Galit especially liked to heap scorn on women who wore larger-sized clothes than she. She made fun of those women and called them lazy. Galit's mother was noticeably overweight, and this caused Galit great anxiety—not about mother's health but about whether Galit would have the same body as her mother in ten or twenty years. "I'd hate myself if I were like that," she whispered to her friends. "How can these women look happy? They should be ashamed of themselves, not happy!"

Galit's scorn toward curvaceous women reflected her own anxiety and her hatred of her own body and its inevitable failings: lumps, bumps, acne, scars, and ripples. Galit feared that she herself might become curvaceous someday, which she equated with the end of men's sexual desires toward her. She mocked such women because they had large endowments in the chest or rear end, which seem to delight and fascinate many men. *Why do men desire fatty tissue?* Galit wondered.

Galit knew that many men were attracted to curvy women, who often seem loving, soft, and gentle. In fact, she heard that such women often were the type men liked to marry. In her high-fashion pretentiousness, Galit thought that thin women ruled the world. She wouldn't accept that men run after gentle-hearted women when that switch goes off in their mind and the men decide to settle down. "He just gave up hope for a quality woman," Galit whispered to her friend when she attended her ex-boyfriend's wedding to a gentle, sweet woman. Galit was too arrogant to be depressed over the wedding.

To Galit, it was simply incomprehensible that a man might choose a soft woman with extra pounds, over her, a woman who was toned and tanned, and who enjoyed facials, manicures, and expensive purses. *He chose the plump one--someone who obviously did not take care of herself—over me.* Galit could not comprehend why. *He probably thinks that because she is such a meek creature, there will always be peace in the home. And he probably thinks that there will never be a threat of other men trying to steal his chunky wife away from him!* she thought. *But he'll tire of having sex with such a woman after the honeymoon ends. He'll realize that she is ugly and seek another lover. I wouldn't want to be her!* So Galit pounded away at the gym every day, thinking that she was preventing such tragic outcomes. *I will keep slim and then I will keep him attracted to me until I tire of him,* she thought.

Galit loved to have influence over men. She had a way of sneaking into men's lives, taking them shopping and helping them select their clothes, giving them advice about women, and telling them what to buy their girlfriends for birthdays and holidays. She threw big parties and always invited some carefully selected single men. She subtly flirted with those handsome, single men after they'd had a drink or two. In response to the thrill of being in the company of such a beautiful woman, they'd start wishing that they could be Galit's boyfriend. This, of course, was exactly the attention she wanted from them. She wanted to feel their desire, even though she had a boyfriend. "I like to know that I have options," she repetitively told herself.

Galit felt a certain deep thrill when she hooked single guys into being dependent on her for social and fashion advice. The excitement was the same feeling she got when she bought an expensive purse, sunglasses, or shirt for herself, a naughty pleasure that she justified by saying to herself, "I deserve it!" She claimed that she bought only high-quality items because they'd last longer. In fact, they did last—in the back of her abundant closet as more trendy items replaced the costly ones.

Despite her shopping addiction, Galit viewed herself as spiritual. In her mind, being spiritual and having status symbols and luxuries were absolutely compatible. There was no conflict between her "self-investment" of buying high-priced, high-fashion items and her commitment to Judaism and her family. She scornfully remarked to people who challenged her to spend less money on clothes, "I don't care what you think, I do what I want." But her shopping fanaticism belied that she did care what others thought. She wanted them to think that she was a high-status person.

Because of all the attention Galit received from the men that she "helped," she could ratchet up the demands and expectations on her boyfriend. Amos held the spot of boyfriend. He was under constant pressure to please her or be replaced. Amos scrambled continuously to do what she asked of him, in hopes of getting a little sexual action from her. Amos derived emotional satisfaction from having such an attractive woman on his arm and in his bed. So he put up with her quirky needs. He knew that many other men wanted Galit, and his pride expanded mightily when they walked around together in public.

Amos was like a salmon in front of a river dam. He always was swimming upstream in his attempts to please Galit, because her current of needs was strong. And Galit never hesitated to ask anything of him:

"Take me to the restaurant that turns at the top of the skyscraper this Saturday." He did.

"Buy me this four-hundred-dollar purse, which I deserve, because I am worth it." He did.

"Buy me those expensive diamond earrings to show me how much you care." He did.

His competitive nature made him do what she "asked" of him, because he wanted to be able to show her off to his friends and make them jealous. She exerted pressure on him to do and buy things because of her competitive nature—she wanted to flaunt his gifts to her friends and make them jealous.

Galit and Amos relished using words like *we* and *us* because they signaled that they were more loved and lovable than others. Being a couple, they also viewed themselves in the category of the "haves," not the "have-nots." The haves were the ones having sex, and the have-nots were assumed not to be having sex.

But people did not know the dirty little secret of their relationship. Sex was a quick thrill for him, and she hardly responded in any way sexually to him, except to say, "You go, boy" and "How was it?" Amos always reached orgasm quickly, without Galit also having an orgasm. She did not care if their sex was over in two minutes because of the psychological satisfaction that she derived from the sexual act. She liked the fact that *she* had a man in her bed and *she* was the one getting sex, not her neighbor or guest.

The best sex that Galit and Amos had was when somebody stayed in the guest bedroom of their apartment. Whether a man or woman, cousin or brother, sister or friend, this couple's competitive side took on a new fervor when they thought that they were the only ones getting sex, when the person in the room next to them was not. They, of course, never seemed to think about the possibility that their guest may have masturbated. But to Galit and Amos, masturbation was not sex and was superbly undesirable compared to the almighty status of being a couple.

"It's expensive to be a person of status," Galit said to frowning Amos as she entered their apartment with several bags of clothes.

"But money flows through you like a flash flood in a desert gorge!" Amos replied coolly.

But Galit never worried. She knew that there would always be more. "The universe provides money when you need it," she consoled her debt-strapped friends who were panicking over paying their next month's rent. They nodded to her as she walked away from them, and then they whispered to each other, "Yes, especially when you have two lovers and ten waiting in line."

"Oh, she is just high maintenance," Galit's long-term friend exclaimed.

"It's more like me maintenance!" another friend responded.

chapter 24

Fatima was embarrassed that she had fallen for a married man. She could not tell anyone about it. But his energy was so sweet, a palpable feeling in the air, whenever they were in bed together. She had gone to his bed in the back of his shop one balmy day when the rosy hues of sunlight bathed the city, when the warm breeze and spicy scents floated through everyone's open windows. She had decided that she was ready for sex, and he was the first man who tried to seduce her with sweet words and flowers. When she nervously hesitated, he held up a condom and said, "Don't worry, you won't get pregnant."

She found the sex part quite easy. Just lick this, stroke that, turn this way. It was all very easy. The tough part was figuring out who her lover was inside, inside that body of his. *What is he thinking? What is he planning? Who is he, really?* she thought as they lay there, exposed and exhausted in post-sex satiety.

The months since their first sex act passed, and Fatima discovered that she was more and more angry at her lover. He seemed to be oblivious to that, and to what she was communicating with her face. He was so lost in the moment, in the pleasure of it all. As they started kissing and hurriedly undressing, she asked him, "The holidays are coming up. When will I see you again?"

He hesitated. "Oh, well, you know. We shall see."

She looked at him and said, "No, tell me when!"

He looked back at her with surprise. "What's the problem? This never mattered to you before!"

"What, am I nothing to you?" Fatima yelled.

She left him lying naked on his bed, the sex act half finished.

Fatima wrote in her diary, *He gets mad at me for attaching to him so closely. But he tells me he won't leave his wife because of their children. He apparently is very attached to his own brood. So how is this different from me attaching to him? Or maybe being needed by his kids is more important to him than my love?*

He is ashamed of me! He is ashamed of being seen with me in public! I want to scream at you, to cry, and to say how unfair it was that you go home to your wife and kids and do not think about me until your next primal urge strikes you!

Fatima slammed her diary shut, bit her lip, and made no noise. She knew that she had allowed this, that she had sought his touch. *That was a very sweet day,* she thought, recalling the first time they were sexually intimate. She sighed at her fortune, or the lack thereof.

Fatima decided to write a letter to him. She bought pink stationery at the store and shoved it into her backpack. After dinner, she snuck into her room and wrote a letter to him: *I want to wrap myself around you—to be a human bow. I give my love like a luscious gift to you, dripping with desire and anticipated pleasure.* She signed her name and kissed it after she put on her best red lipstick. She sprayed the letter with perfume, and then she mailed it to him.

She waited for a response, any response. Weeks later, her best friend whispered to her about what happened. His wife had intercepted the letter and read it. They got into a huge fight, screaming loudly enough that the neighbors looked out at their apartment. He ran out of the house, and that was all that the neighbors saw. Fatima smiled to herself. *The letter might be working.*

Indeed, the sex had been the easy part. He wanted her, she consented, and it was done. But a relationship was the hard part. Growing up, she had listened to her aunts and cousins talk about that. They also talked about how it was especially difficult to be the second wife of a Muslim man. *But this was a secret affair,* she thought, *so it should've been a little easier for me, because I did not have to deal with all the social complications of interacting with his family and friends. Nor did I have to compete with a second wife for his love.*

One day, he called her. He wanted to meet at a coffee shop. *He's choosing me!* she thought. And she ran to meet him. Their meeting ended with a coupling in his closed store. *He's come back to me!* Fatima thought triumphantly.

Fatima sent daily e-mail and text messages to her lover. He always responded with a friendly greeting and a joke or two. *I like it when he sends me a text or e-mail. Especially when it makes a beep, beep in class. The students look at me with smiles or envy. I text him back, typing on my phone hidden behind a book. I feel very naughty! And then when I run to him after my classes end for the day, I am naughty!* she wrote in her diary.

Fatima continued bedding her married lover, but she started formulating a plan. She decided that education was her only ticket out of her suffocating life. *I will pawn all his gifts and buy a plane ticket out. Maybe I'll go to England, or United Arab Emirates. Wherever I can get a scholarship for the university!* She started planning her escape. Every week, she sent applications to any university that had scholarships for international students. Every time her lover visited, he gave her little gifts—sometimes nice ones, like a little gold heart locket, but other times thoughtless gifts, like a few roses past their prime or some chocolates melted by the sun. She made sure the sex was especially bad after those gifts. Occasionally, he brought her a substantial gift, but never money. *If he gave me money, I'd feel like a prostitute, and that'd cheapen our sex.* Fatima liked her plan to pawn his gifts. *He'd be mad at me if he knew I always got rid of his gifts.*

Even at the young age of sixteen, Fatima knew that money was essential in this life. *The gifts he gives me will pay for my freedom and passage out of this country,* she thought. Of course, she did not tell her lover about her plans. She was sure that he did not want her to succeed, because that meant she would leave him. *But he can't stop me,* she thought.

One day, Fatima saw her lover with his kids and his wife at the market. He just nodded to her and kept walking. No smile, no other greeting. It was like she was invisible.

What about all the pledges of love that he gave me in bed? As she stood, astonished and immobile, she realized that his whispered words in bed had only one purpose: to make her keep running to him. *He likes me clinging to him, wanting him, obeying him, pleasing him! But that's it. He doesn't think about me. I won't take it anymore! Today, today I am free of you!* she angrily thought as she watched him walk away, his brood following after him like ducklings.

chapter 25

SOLOMON ENJOYED BEING KING and the attention inherent in such an occupation. Men bowed before him, acknowledging that Solomon was divinely appointed and represented King David's lineage. The women also bowed before him, but Solomon preferred them more prostrate and subordinate. He loved female affection and attention—he thought there was nothing sweeter.

Shirit was a gentle young woman who was sixteen years old. She had moist brown eyes that expressed a soft wonder at the world. Solomon stopped to talk with her when he saw her at an olive tree in the village square. He suddenly connected with her eyes and felt like he saw past her body into an unknown space—like he was falling into that space through her eyes. He did not understand what had happened, but he thought it was a divine sign. He ran after her when she turned to go home. *I want this one!* he thought as he pursued her down a dusty road to her home, where he asked her father for her hand in marriage.

The night of the marriage was a joyous one. Solomon, as always, was enraptured and enthralled by the presence of a new lover. He liked to place his indelible stamp on a woman—taking her as a virgin and bringing her into his collected family. As usual, his other wives did not want to see the lavish wedding ceremony—it created enormous jealousy and anger among them.

It was known throughout the land that King Solomon had

his preferences and that he would invite a woman to visit him until she conceived a child. After delivery of her child, Solomon rarely summoned her back to him. He constantly had new offers and new women to choose from. Some women could not be consoled by his practices. They cried every day and refused to return to Solomon on the rare days when he asked them to return. But Solomon never knew about such reactions. To him, his arrangements with women had mutual benefits. He promised the women care for life in return for interludes with him. He thought it was a fair exchange.

A few months later, they thought Shirit was pregnant, so they sent her from Solomon's chambers to the women's quarters. She started taking daily walks around the palace. One day, Shirit ran into a childhood friend, who was visiting the palace as a soldier in charge of the biggest unit in Judah. Solomon watched their interaction from the privacy of his quarters.

From his window, Solomon could see them talking and laughing in the courtyard. They were chattering, gesturing with their hands, and looking at each other closely. He felt anger and jealousy over the laughter and the playful joy between these two. He wanted it to stop immediately. He yelled for his advisor.

"Shirit is mine, and she should be veiled and hidden from other males immediately. Do this for my sake! She already has my child!" he roared. Solomon angrily told his advisor to take Shirit back to the women's quarters. Solomon then ran out of the palace and rode his royal horse off into the desert. Three of his military leaders rode after him. He kept thinking, *I do not want to be like my father. No, I cannot and will not. God help me.*

Solomon rode furiously for several hours, and his leaders tried to keep up with him. His eyes were rimmed with red and his face dusted with the fine grit of the desert. He repetitively whispered to himself through his clenched teeth, "God, I beg you to stop me from slaughtering this man myself in the courtyard." Galloping over the dunes, Solomon seethed in anger and rode chaotically, no destination as a goal.

chapter 26

GALIT AND AMOS OFTEN invited guests to stay with them in Galit's apartment, which was now "theirs." Galit liked when people, especially Amos's brother, visited them and stayed over, sleeping on the couch. He obviously desired Galit and wanted the life that Amos had. And of course, when Amos's brother was around, Galit and Amos made more noise during sex at night. They felt naughty having sex with someone in the next room, who could hear their grunts and moans. "He wants what we have!" Galit whispered to Amos as she wrestled him down into the fluffy pillows.

In the morning, Galit and Amos were all smiles as they served their guest breakfast. No words needed to be spoken, because they had made sure to vocalize their conquest of each other loudly enough for their guest to hear through the walls. They found it very exhilarating for their sex life.

When Galit's baby arrived, her competitive nature got an additional boost. Now she had little Anat, with her beautiful blue eyes, as a source of compliments and attention from others. At the market, Galit paraded little Anat around like she was the most remarkable parent in the world. Her baby sling displayed

Anat face-forward so everyone could see her large eyes, toothless smile, and cute layers of baby fat. Pedestrians stopped in their tracks when they saw the slender, attractive woman with the beautiful child. "Just like out of a magazine!" they whispered about Galit and Anat.

But Amos was not sure if Anat was his daughter. She looked so different from him, a little darker in skin tone. Galit never answered him when he asked her who Anat's father was. He stopped asking. But he didn't care much because their sexual impulses increased with little Anat in the other room. "We shouldn't be doing this!" They laughed, but they did not stop. Anat laughed and imitated the noises that they were making. They said to each other, "Anat is too young to understand" and continued in their sexual entwining.

Galit took particular pride in buying Anat the "best" baby clothes. She could only buy the clothing from expensive stores, made by top designers, using the finest fabrics, such as organic cotton, with imported wooden buttons handmade by workers from the Andes. Of course, Galit fed Anat only the best food, always organic, and no refined sugar. She even gave organic food to her cats.

Galit only bought the best products and designer clothes for herself. "I need this," she told herself to justify an extravagant purchase. "I have to be the best, so I have to buy the best," she whispered to herself. She thought that she was the most beautiful, sexiest woman, the most fashionable, the hippest, the best sister, the best daughter, the best friend, the best lover. "I am Galit. I deserve it!" she said to herself as she purchased a six-hundred-dollar orange leather purse.

Galit was sophisticated enough that she never overtly demanded anything from her lover or family. But she was a master manipulator, suggesting that she needed certain large gifts from her parents and lover and knowing that they'd never say "no" to her. They reflexively reacted, giving her whatever she asked, no matter the cost. She also dropped hints that "good parents would ..." or "a good boyfriend would ..." as little bones of encouragement.

"Always the best" was Galit's motto. "Everything has to be the best—food, clothes, family ... mine is the best," she said to herself. "Life is one big, fat competition, and I am in front of the pack!" she exclaimed to herself while examining her slender profile in the mirror.

chapter 27

RACHEL HEARD ABOUT ANOTHER suicide bombing that had just happened a few hours ago. She wondered, *What is it with this land of Israel?* She walked around the Old City of Jerusalem, observing religions of all colors and stripes being practiced there. *Many think that Jerusalem is the spiritual capital of the world, the vortex of the spiritual past, present, and future. But how do you explain all the violence? This is opposite of spirituality!* she thought.

Rachel wandered around the streets of Jerusalem, looking more at people's faces, body language, and social interactions than at the shop windows and their wares. She was curious about what drove people to do and say things. Her psychotherapist's inquisitiveness came out. *How did they bring rational order into this hot, dustbowl of a land?* she wondered.

On a bus ride to Jerusalem, Rachel met some Jewish settlers. They told her they had never traveled outside of Israel. "Why do that?" they said when she asked them whether they ever wanted to travel around the world. And they told her that they did not like going on even occasional trips outside Jerusalem. They especially avoided Tel Aviv, which they called a "free-for-all chaos," and "a land of Jewish lost souls."

Rachel could not understand the settlers' mentality. *Do they really think that they are in the center of the universe and that there is no reason to travel outside Israel?* Like a good scientific clinician, Rachel started asking the same questions of other settlers she met. She waited for the inevitable moment that they turned to her with a puzzled look that said, "Why even ask?"

I wonder whether they feel threatened by the thought of leaving hearth and home and venturing into foreign lands? Are they threatened by new ideas? How can you not desire to see and hear new ideas, cultures, and ways of living? I don't think I could ever say that I have everything I need here, no matter where I lived. I don't think that'd ever be true, because I'm too curious about the world.

Sitting beside her on a city bus, one visitor to Jerusalem proclaimed to Rachel, "I don't feel the same isolation as I do in America. In Israel, I feel bonded and connected with people." Rachel nodded her head in agreement with him as he talked and gestured excitedly. She opened the bus window and leaned away from him, trying to escape the garlic odor from his mouth. Once he exited the bus, Rachel sat silently, waiting for the central bus station stop. *It's really all the same,* she thought. *People in America, Europe, and Jerusalem sit quietly in buses, wrapped up in their thoughts, fidgeting with their cell phones, music, newspapers, or books, or catching a little sleep before their destination.* She looked around at the solemn, distracted, tired faces. *And we all feel awkward around each other!*

Rachel walked down the street slowly to let the others who had exited the bus push into the bus station. She chuckled after two women walked past, chatting excitedly in New York accents. They were both dressed from head to toe in what looked like the most expensively made layered linen dresses, common among Orthodox women. *No doubt New York liberals!* she chuckled to herself. She imagined that the women wanted to show solidarity with "their" people, and so as soon as they arrived they took a taxi to a small boutique, known for carrying the top Israeli designers. They'd emerge after a few hours with rectangular paper bags with twine handles filled with tissue paper–wrapped dresses made from the finest linen, dyed various shades of purple. Their next stop would be to buy Italian sandals to complete their outfits. Rachel laughed at her imagining of their shopping trip. *Ah, but they forget to cover their heads, which is a dead giveaway. But maybe their feminist views prevent them from covering their heads!* she thought, chuckling at the idea of New York liberals trying so hard to fit in with the natives.

She continued imagining the women's lives. *No doubt they thoroughly enjoy the Hanukkah feasts and Jewish Passover and abundantly use the phrases like "My heritage, our heritage" and "we, the chosen people."* Rachel imagined a family scene in which a child asked them to state the Ten Commandments and the two women couldn't recite them to the child. *And no doubt they expected to be loved and embraced by their Eretz Yisrael. They probably think, "These people must love me, because I am one of them," even if they are annoying New Yorkers!* She laughed to herself.

Rachel sat on a number nineteen Jerusalem bus in an aisle seat reading a book. She glanced at movement beside her and looked up at an angry young woman's face. Her head was wrapped in a headscarf, and she wore long sleeves and a long skirt, the tradition for Orthodox women. The woman suddenly exclaimed something in Hebrew, stood up, and pushed herself out to the aisle. Rachel was saying, "I don't understand." Rachel's book, her bag, and her scarf were all scattered on the dirty floor of the bus. Rachel stood there in astonishment, not knowing what happened, nor why. She gathered her things and then moved to the window seat.

The angry young woman stood in the area without seats, talking and gesturing to an older woman about taking the vacant seat. Rachel finally understood that the Orthodox woman expected Rachel to give up her seat for the elderly woman, whom she had not noticed. And despite the Orthodox woman's furtive gesturing, the elderly lady did not take the seat.

Rachel puzzled over this, thinking, *If that is what religious practices do to you, then something is wrong! Polite manners and giving one's seat to an elderly person are good in any culture. But it is a whole other matter to do it aggressively, angrily, and blaming me. Is that what her orthodoxy does to her? Make her rigid and livid?* she thought. *But what am I thinking? Maybe it's not about her orthodoxy? Maybe she's just a pushy person who happens to be Orthodox?*

As Rachel walked home, she remembered the crisis of faith she had when she was younger. *To this day, I still wonder which brand of Christianity I should follow, since I disagree with several ideas, no matter which type of Christianity I study,* she thought as she opened the door of the small room she was renting in Jerusalem on King George Street. "Does this question really matter?" she challenged herself. "It matters to me!" she answered as she plunked down her plastic grocery bags and filled the electric tea kettle with water.

Rachel thought about when she was younger, how she'd wanted to be around people who followed rules. Though she was fiercely independent, Rachel liked rules and believed in the value of moral rules. *Rules can insert some rationality when strong physiological and emotional urges crash over us in waves. And rules provided structure in a chaotic world,* she thought.

As Rachel grew older, her question became, "Which or whose moral rules to follow?" She studied the religious system of her youth and found it flawed. So she sought a religious system that made more rational sense. Then she sought a system that was democratic and allowed a variety of religious interpretations. She could not find that system. *All religious systems must defend their own beliefs. They disappear when there are too many questions and doubts. Just like interpersonal relationships,* she thought.

Rachel's family and her church treated other religions like viruses spreading spiritual plagues. But she was curious and started studying the claims of religions like a budding scientist. Because religious systems were not fact-oriented but based on tradition, stories, writings, ideas, concepts, and perceptions, Rachel decided that her search was too broad. So she focused only on Christian theology, which still turned out to be an immense task. Delving into the realm of theology made her slip into an existential crisis when she saw how branches within Christianity were divided over words and their interpretation. *But what should I believe in?* she thought, panicking at the thought that there were really no final answers to many ultimate questions. *Maybe it takes greater faith to be outside religious systems, because no group is buttressing your faith? If I let go of everything I know, I have to walk blindly into the unknown. That takes bravery, because everything is tenuous!*

One night, she decided to challenge God. "I always believed in the existence of You, God. But I want to know if and how You interact with us humans! God, show me that you exist!" Rachel declared to the night sky.

chapter 28

From the time he was a young boy, King Solomon had always believed in the existence of the Most High God, who was known by many names, including the God of Abraham, El Shaddai. For decades, Solomon's father, King David, had spoken so passionately about God that it was hard for Solomon not to believe. Solomon loved his father deeply and had reverence for the power that David exuded. But Solomon did not seem to experience God in an emotional way as his father did. King David seemed to be enraptured by God and wrote many songs about him. Solomon preferred reading the words of the sages and understanding life and its mysteries.

As a young boy, Solomon liked to hear the stories about how God saved his people from the many armies wanting to extinguish or subjugate them. He especially liked to hear how the will of the people of Israel would not be broken. As he grew, Solomon spent many hours in the synagogue, listening to stories of survival and the erudite reasoning of the rabbis. But then Solomon found women.

At first, young Solomon chased after pretty girls, who shyly withdrew from him when he stood directly in front of them and tried to speak into their bowed faces. They would not look straight at him. Like captured animals, they averted their focus, quickly looking to the left or right. Then, one summer day, under the sun's searing rays, Solomon met a woman who not only looked at him directly but spoke to him in soft, sing-song tones. She invited him to her tent for some water. He willingly accepted the invitation. The water was never drunk, but he drank mightily of love and left her tent a man.

After his first intimate contact with a woman, Solomon began seeking a replication of his first time of ecstasy. *Love is challenging, like a riddle to solve,* he thought. He started learning who provided it and under what circumstances. *There is always a reason women offer such close access to their beings. I have to find out why,* he thought to himself. *It's either attraction to me or they want security from me.* But from the time when Solomon started noticing women, his father told him, "Honor God and stay away from married women!"

As a young man, Solomon started writing poetry, as did his father. But the content was different—Solomon's favorite topics were women and people, while David wrote about God. Solomon was inspired by women—their smiles, their laughter, their long hair that flowed with the desert wind, their loving embraces and warm eyes. *So different from me. Joy on earth! Nothing sweeter in this world,* Solomon thought.

King David taught young Solomon many stories about other nations and their laws, their practices, and their strength on the battlefield. He also talked about how other nations had temple prostitutes and that men went to the temples to have sex in the name of the gods. Their sex was equated with prayer to their gods. Solomon was curious about this practice and asked his father to tell him more about it. King David first recoiled at his questions, and then with a stern face, he instructed Solomon. "First, it is not befitting for a king to visit temple prostitutes, because they are foreigners and could possibly trap you in those moments of vulnerability. Second, such acts also break the first commandment given to Moses and our forefathers: Have no other gods before me."

King David warned his son, "Sex is not a prayer to our God. While it can be heavenly, it is a form of adoring another human—loving them, seeking them, embracing them, uniting with them. And that is permitted. But it is not a god-worshipping act, because the focus of sex is not our God but the woman. Never confuse the two!"

To Solomon, sex was simple: a beautiful act that made him feel very close to a woman. But it was over quickly and the feeling passed, and then he had many things to do, people to see, and advice to give. Solomon once told his advisor Ahishar, "Sweet flavors fade in a few minutes. And my tongue develops an aversion to a food after consuming too much at one sitting. Just like women. My taste for her rapidly fades. And then I have to find a new woman." Ahishar, looking stunned and uncomfortable, quickly excused himself from Solomon's presence.

Most people feared Solomon. Yet numerous women wanted to be his lover. So he had ample selection and abundant access. It was as easy for Solomon to get a new lover as picking ripe tomatoes from the vine in the summertime. But then they clung to him like vines after sex. Solomon never understood women's reactions about sex. They often got weepy with Solomon after the sex act. This made him angry, so he sent them away and did not want to be around them. Sometimes his lover tried to walk beside him, in order to show the other women that he was *hers*. But he was king of the land, so he just whispered to Ahishar and she was taken away from him.

In the middle of the night when he could not sleep, Solomon started thinking about his strong attraction to women and the repulsion for them that soon followed. He did not know who to ask for advice. His father, King David, was no longer living. But even if he were, Solomon doubted whether his advice would have helped much, for King David was moody and often depressed. King David had long ago given up pursuing women, especially after his bitter lesson with Bathsheba. Instead, David chased after his enemies and conquered them on the battlefield. Solomon was peace-loving and wanted nothing to do with war. Of course, he was strict about having good defenses throughout his country and was proud to support his military men.

But the chase Solomon most enjoyed was running after a woman. Inevitably, she responded willingly and with delight at his attention. No woman ever refused Solomon. But of course, Solomon did not run after every woman. He did not want to be with a married woman. *I don't want to be like my father,* he thought. *And as king, I need to set an example.*

His advisors always made sure that the women King Solomon had contact with were unmarried. His advisors also did not allow their own wives to meet him, because they knew what a powerful attraction the king was to women. Solomon's strength and charisma made most women melt before him, as well as his status as king of the land. His advisors also would not allow his daughters to see Solomon, because they knew what might happen.

But no woman who chased after King Solomon ever thought about how difficult it would be to live with hundreds of other women in his women's quarters. The most important thing was to be with the king of the land and to have his child. And maybe even to be his queen.

chapter 29

GALIT AND ANAT, WITH Amos in tow, attended the wedding of Galit's cousin. Galit started taking pictures the moment she entered the wedding celebration. She handed Amos her purse and ran off with little Anat in her arms.

Amos sat at the bar and talked with an old army buddy the whole evening. He watched his girlfriend Galit run around with a camera stuck to her face. He started laughing. "Funny how a hundred years ago, there were no videos and few cameras, and people still enjoyed themselves," Amos said. "Now we have to document every living moment for fear the moment will be forgotten as not important, or else we don't think it's a special moment! Or maybe we think *we* will be forgotten?" Amos asked his buddy without giving him time to respond. "We are so busy documenting and looking good that we forget to relate to others!" Amos said with a slur, a beer in his hand. His army friend mumbled an agreement and then stumbled toward the bathroom.

Amos watched his girlfriend again. Galit kept chasing little Anat around, not noticing when she ran into people because she only saw where she was going through the distorted view of the camera lens. Galit took pictures of Anat everywhere: coated with a piece of cake that she was eating, running around the dance floor in her pink dress with a tulle skirt and sparkles, pushing through the adults, yelling her ABCs right in the middle of the dance floor. Galit kept laughing and clicking photographs of Anat's bouncy moves in every shade of light and from every angle.

The next day, Amos received a copy of Galit's most prized photo. It was little Anat in pink standing in front of the newly married couple. In the picture, the couple's faces were cut off and only the white wedding dress and black tuxedo were visible from the neck down. But in the center of the picture stood Anat, all smiles and curly hair: the center of the universe.

Amos's mother Netti loved to babysit Anat. "She is the smartest, cutest little girl," she gushed as she plopped her things down in Amos and Galit's apartment and hugged Anat.

Netti, a plump Israeli woman born in Be'er Sheva to a Jewish mother and Arab-Christian father, had straight, jet-black hair and flashing black eyes heavily outlined in black eyeliner. Netti was an extrovert, a social butterfly, and a gossip, all rolled into a plump package of mobile energy. She liked to spend her days running around talking to people, collecting gossip, and planning the next party. She had not changed her bobbed haircut for forty years. She carefully hooked her hair behind her right ear at least twelve times per hour. She walked as if she were a beautiful woman who should be admired by all.

Netti's lover was an Ethiopian Jew who immigrated to Israel in 1985 when the Mossad coordinated an operation to rescue as many Jews as possible from Africa. He was a tall man, dark-skinned like roasted cocoa beans, with a bright smile full of shiny white teeth and a warm face. He sported long dreadlocks that went halfway down his back. His muscles rippled with tension as he sauntered down the hot and dusty streets of Tel Aviv. He was quite a regal sight to behold, and women always enjoyed his presence, both in and outside of their beds. Though Netti was a high-anxiety person with a mouth that spun sentences like the fastest woolen mill and who swore as thick and deep as a sewer, she had an intensity and confidence about her that attracted men.

When Netti turned on the charm and flirted with a man, there were moments when she could be quite charming and seductive. But in essence she was a hard woman. Her lover, in his mild, marijuana-hazed state, did not notice her anger and frustration at daily life. He drifted through the room, radiating the love of Rasta, not bothered by her irritated frenzy. In fact, he had a calming effect on Netti. All it took to calm her down was for him to encircle her waist and start kissing her neck. That took her to a different level, if not another world, altogether, causing her voice to soften and her womanly honey to be available to the bee collector.

On Netti's bedroom wall hung a picture of Marilyn Monroe, looking sultry while reclining on a couch. When Amos studied it, he wondered, *Does she need this picture as an inspiration or a reminder of how to act beautiful and sexy?* He did not like how his mother acted around men. *She was too old for that*, he thought. Netti liked to tell Amos the story of when she dated an Air Force pilot while she was in high school, before she met her ex-husband. Amos pictured his mother arrogantly walking around with her pilot in tow, bragging to her friends that she had a date with him on Saturday evening.

Netti flamboyantly bragged to her friends, "My family is the best in the world!" She kept doing so even after she divorced her husband. Netti never let anyone other than her immediate family babysit her children. It was the same with her granddaughter Anat. No babysitter could ever meet Netti's standards. "Nobody can love my children and grandchildren as much as I do!" she earnestly explained.

Since Galit was young, she relished using the term *us*. First, it was with her family. And then she discovered boys. In her quick successions of boyfriends through school, she particularly savored using the term *my boyfriend*. It was a status badge to her.

But having the status of "Galit's boyfriend" was hard work. The boy had to struggle to pass all of her "must" tests—"You must take me out on a date to the movies"; "You must buy me a big birthday gift"; "You must call me every day." These "musts" were never directly verbalized to the hapless boy, just hinted at until he did what she wanted. If he didn't, he would be de-boyfriended.

Galit knew how to play one boy off another and bring out their competitive natures. At a young age, she understood the delicate balance between control and pressure. She knew how stroke the boys' egos until they obeyed her carefully disguised commands. The "velvet prima-donna" was a nickname a group of girls gave Galit during high school, because she was such a smooth, silky kind of girl who knew how to squeeze out what she wanted from practically anyone. These girls laughed at Galit's game and mimicked her manipulations and her arrogant way of strolling, which not only signaled her attitude "I am privileged" but also "you want me so bad, boys, and I know it."

Guys were clueless to Galit's game. But the girls understood that Galit was capitalizing on what guys wanted. "She will be a great businesswoman someday," they joked among themselves. Her friends had plenty to laugh about when the topic of Galit and guys came up, but they were envious of her great charisma with men.

When Galit closed in on a new boy, the girls laughed because "Galit was in heat," and they observed, "The poor boy will be wrung dry." Sometimes they watched with amazement, and some jealousy, how Galit drew a boy in. He came eagerly running to her at the slightest snap of her manicured fingers and the flick of her expensively treated, streaked, and styled blond hair. Galit then used the poor boy as a tool to gain and maintain the attention of the man she really wanted. This scenario played out with many men in many situations. In the end, there was always a hurt boy, a triumphant Galit, and a more attentive boyfriend. It was classic love-triangle manipulation. But in their haze of glory over being able to walk with and talk to Galit, these boys never understood it.

Not many girls truly liked Galit. But they grouped around her, drawn to her emanations of power and popularity. Galit knew how to make the girls feel comfortable. After all, she knew that a cluster of girls boosted her status as a likeable and important person. Girls easily flocked to her with their school gossip, ogling over the latest high-priced clothing lines, relishing tidbits about celebrity dating and mating. Nothing was off limits to them, and they felt entitled to everything expensive and fashionable.

Galit and her friends spent hours at the mall at least three days a week. Grabbing their lattes and frappuccinos, they chatted about boys, clothes, parties, and music as they clicked down the mall corridors, hunting for the next sexy blouse or outrageous shoes. They did not view their behavior as a shopping addiction as their bill-paying fathers did. It was just fun and something they had to do. They used their negotiation skills to get their fathers to pay off their balances. After all, they explained to their fathers, these purchases were "must haves" and non-negotiable.

They felt alive at malls: the thrill of the hunt, the feel-good moment when they discovered a newly minted fashion item, and the sense of naughtiness over the high price they were paying. They scoured the malls to be ahead of others in modeling new trends. They also scanned the environment for terrorists and for fashion violations.

Galit and her friends never shopped at low-priced discount stores. They justified their need for high-priced clothes by claiming that they shopped for quality. In their minds, "only the best" meant shopping only at expensive stores. With great enthusiasm, they exclaimed gleefully to themselves, "And we deserve no less!"

chapter 30

AFTER A FEW HOLIDAYS passed without Fatima seeing or hearing from her lover, she decided to contact him, because she was worried whether he was okay. He wrote her back immediately, exclaiming how glad he was to hear from her and saying that he had wanted to give her some breathing room. They e-mailed back and forth for twenty minutes. He then proposed that they meet for coffee that very day. He said he would cancel his appointments and close his shop to come talk with her.

Fatima signed off her e-mail feeling triumphant. *Look what he does in order to see me!* she thought to herself as she ran to her room to change clothes and put on makeup.

They met a dark coffee house on a back street near his store. He talked quickly, staring directly in her eyes and smiling. How she had hungered for this moment. *He needs me! He misses me!* she joyously thought. They finished their espressos and left to go to his small shop. Of course, sex happened.

After a few hours had sweetly passed, he relaxed in a chair with a cup of coffee. She decided to confront him. "So when are you going to leave your wife?" she asked, looking at him as she sat on the small bed in his back office. He stuttered, stumbled, and then said, "Fatima, please! You know it is hard with kids. Divorce scars them for the rest of their lives." She looked down at the teacup in her hands and frowned.

He continued, "It is God's will that I stay with my wife. Neither she, nor the kids, can live without me."

Fatima exploded with anger. "Is it God's will that you screw around with me and then go home to your wife?"

Fatima grabbed a handful of big round soft bagels off the shoddy table and threw three at him in a row. He lifted his arms up in defense. She yelled, "You are evil, not godly!" She ran out the door and turned down a narrow street. With tears streaming down her face, she ran past people shopping at food stalls. She did not see them looking at her and gesturing to each other.

As Fatima sat in class trying to listen to her teacher, her mind traveled back to the room in Jerusalem where she first learned about sex. She remembered the dirt, dust, heat, noise, and frenetic daily life that circled around that small room where she met her lover. She remembered how he felt in her arms and how he'd smell: the sweat, the cologne, the smell of sex. She remembered that they lost track of time as they dove into the sexual stimuli and ecstasy. *Ah, how I loved you during those days*, she thought. *But now you are dead to me and I will not contact you anymore.* She flipped her notebook open to a blank page and hurriedly scrawled:

> I don't want
> To see you
> Anymore
> Because
> The desire
> Is too sharp
> And the pain
> Increases
> Fourscore
> When I
> Picture

How you
Touch her.
I will not,
Cannot,
Share
My body
My heart
With you
Anymore.
No more, no more.

When Fatima returned to her room that evening, she reread her poem. She angrily ripped the paper from the notebook and shoved it into her desk drawer, scratching her hand as she threw it in. She started crying. She sat on the floor holding her injured hand and wept. *I loved you. Doesn't that matter to you?* she thought. She stood up and then sat down on her bed and cried some more. She dozed off and woke a few hours later with a sense of peace. She told herself, *Don't fool yourself. If you don't sleep with him, he will find someone else to cheat with. If he really wanted to marry you and if he had a moral conscience, he would've filed for a divorce a long time ago.*

A few weeks and many tears later, Fatima stood browsing titles in a musty bookstore. She pulled out a book called *The Feminine Mystique* by Betty Freidan. She started skimming the chapters and then read a few paragraphs. She stood paralyzed. In those pages, she read the stories of thousands of American women. They explained how they felt trapped in their lives and felt that their lives of serving their husbands and children had no meaning. And they felt that they were denied any freedom of thought or choice. Fatima was astonished. *It's like they're speaking to me!* With shaking hands, she bought the book with the last coins in her purse and ran home. She devoured the hundreds of pages in a few days.

Once Fatima finished *The Feminine Mystique*, she began reading more and more books and articles on feminism. They explained so much. So many of the secret thoughts she had were expressed there by other women. *But I still can't share these thoughts with my family or friends. They want to protect the status quo. They'd try to talk me out of reading this stuff! But I won't let them. It's too interesting!*

Fatima thought that the phenomena about American women described in Friedan's book were also true among Middle Eastern Muslim women. She pulled out her diary and started writing. *Our chances of getting an advanced education are near zero, unless we want to fight the harassment and ridicule to get a degree. How fair is that for women? And in the Middle East, we women have even less of a valued status to men because in many countries, a man can marry several of us at a time but not vice versa. If you do not suit him or obey him, he can toss you out the door and bring in another wife within a day or two. This leaves no room for negotiation,* Fatima wrote.

Fatima thought about her mother. Najib was surrounded by her children, her spouse, and many friends. But Najib seemed very fragile and, at times, frightfully alone but unwilling to admit it. *My mother is like many of the older women in the community. Family is the primary structure for meaning in their lives. Yet they are not happy! Most of these wives endlessly complain to their female social circle about their husband's small offenses. Even about the men who were faithful and would never cheat. But these women are probably petty about everything. They probably nag their husbands incessantly at home,* Fatima wrote in her diary.

The men who are criticized are often decent guys, but they may be slightly clueless. These critical women irritate me. Why can't they appreciate that they have someone? And what the men have done for them? And that the men stay with them? What's more ironic is that these women attack the very system that gives them meaning and security. That must mean that they are not happy, she wrote.

I don't like the bossy women who think they are wise because they have five or ten kids. They are everywhere here. You cannot get away from them. They believe that everything that they say is valuable and right. They seem perfectly happy to express their opinions to others ad nauseum, without ever slowing their mouths down enough to think about how critical, negative, or petty their thoughts are. If I were a man, I wouldn't want to live with such a woman! Fatima wrote.

Fatima thought about what many feminists said about sex and kept writing. *Some feminists proclaimed that women have the right to sexual exploration just like a man, and that women should have sex without a relationship as a means of expressing female power. I don't like these ideas, because it seems to be emotional masochism to me, not an expression of liberation. To me, sexual liberation means having an equal value with a man in a marriage, not one-fourth value from sharing your husband with three other wives. So maybe that makes me a conservative feminist?* She laughed to herself as she finished writing that sentence.

If I am very, very honest with myself, I admit that I want attention from a man. But I want one who loves me passionately and exclusively, for both my mind and body. All around me, I can't find any examples of this. I see no couples that seem equally balanced and equally enthusiastic about being with each other. It always seems like one is more invested in the other. One always seems to chase the other. While the man may pursue the woman sexually, it seems like the woman pursues her husband emotionally, she wrote in her diary. *All know is that I need to carefully evaluate the character of the man whom I let into my bed.*

Fatima thought about her own mistakes of the past year. She realized that in her affair with a married man, she was really just a sex object, like many feminists wrote about. She noted in her diary, *But it did not feel like he was using me, because he kept saying my name and saying how he loved me. So how was I just a sex object?*

She laid down her diary and leaned back on her bed, thinking about her lover. She pictured him with his glasses, hairy chest, rolls of fat, body odor, and she scoffed. *Many men here are hypocrites. They sleep around with young and old women, but they won't let their daughters date!*

She wrote in her diary, *He was two words: greedy, arrogant. To think that he could control the hearts of two women, make them both run after his love. One is not enough. Greedy indeed!*

chapter 31

SOLOMON LOVED WOMEN. THIS was obvious to his advisors, his family, and most of his kingdom. While he exhibited solemn rationality and logic when he held court, he became a witty, attentive, and charming male once he left his court. Women followed him out of his court into the street, signaling their interests to him with their eyes and wry smiles.

Solomon often shrugged off the accusations of men who claimed that he was stealing from them and living a life of extreme excess. Solomon easily and good-naturedly responded to these attacks with detailed explanations of how and where he spent the money given to him by people across the land. He knew that men accused him of theft only because they were jealous of his great fortune. Sometimes Solomon was bemused by other men's jealousy. *But I am special. I am appointed by God to build His temple for worship. And I am building the temple.*

In court, he watched with detached amusement how new women begged him every day for entrance into his life and quarters. *Like I am a charity provider!* he thought disdainfully. But in the evenings, he enjoyed bestowing all sorts of fineries and delicacies on his women. They danced with delight and chattered like little children. He liked to see them so excited and happy.

One night after dinner, Solomon silently looked at the huge number of women grouped around his tables. He watched their fluid beauty as they ate, talked, took care of children, and laughed. *Not one that I want to talk with,* he thought.

He walked back to his quarters and composed a message to the queen of Sheba, asking her to visit in the fall. *The temple should be finished by then,* he thought. "I have to meet this woman," he muttered, wiping the corner of his mouth with his sleeve.

The next day in court, King Solomon stood up and declared to everyone, "Serving God is the only important thing in life!" He saw people whisper among themselves and look at him. Solomon continued, "Men, all is dust!" He continued his explanation after scanning the puzzled faces around him. "It comes from dust and returns to dust!" And then he heartily chuckled, thinking they were still babes in their understanding of the world.

He looked around the room. Nobody was smiling. It was silent except for the chattering of children who were playing outside. He stood up and said, "Get going! Let us finish the temple!" Solomon ran out into the sunshine and yelled to the marketplace, "Let us finish the temple!"

Solomon ran to the temple and gave orders and commands to everyone who crossed his path. He became angrier and angrier with his advisors, snapping at them. His advisors whispered together in the corner, looking his way. They sent for the prophet Nathan and told him what they saw. He fasted and prayed for a day and then returned to them.

Nathan said to a small group of priests and advisors, "The God of Abraham is a God of Mercy. But He is the God Most High who told Israel not to worship other gods. Solomon is worshipping Molech and Ashtoret. He will soon know the consequences if he does not stop."

They fell silent at Nathan's words. After Nathan left, they whispered, "What will become of King Solomon?" Then they scattered to tell their friends the news.

chapter 32

MOSHE AND GALIT MET for the first time at a coffee house in Tel Aviv, after chatting online for a few days through a Jewish dating site. Moshe thought, *Here's a girl who looks normal and who has great hair and a tight body.*

Galit thought, *Here's a guy who looks nice, like a momma's boy.*

They chatted for several hours, comparing notes about schools, military service, and families. They laughed together and smiled a lot. As they talked, Galit leaned forward in such a way that her breasts flopped on the table before her, like a platter of food served before Moshe. Her low-cut shirt gave him a tasty view of the edges of her round, firm breasts.

When it came time to say good-bye because the café was closing, Moshe suggested that they take a walk. Galit agreed. The fall air had a chilly edge to it, so Moshe took the opportunity to loan Galit his jacket. She had intentionally worn a spaghetti-strap shirt, knowing that guys like to put their jackets around their dates. Moshe used the movement to keep his arm around her and pull the jacket back around her when it began slipping off.

They strolled aimlessly for an hour around the dirty, busy streets of Tel Aviv and then ended up in front of Moshe's apartment. He invited her up for a "coffee" and she said yes. She said, "Only because I am quite cold and need to warm up." She knew men and understood that this was Moshe's tactical move to get her upstairs.

Once inside, Moshe continued with his strategy and offered her a cup of coffee. "Well, actually, it's too late for coffee. I need to get up early in the morning," she said, looking at him with glinting eyes. He stood looking at her awkwardly and responded with a half-smile. Then she jumped him, encircling him with her arms and legs. They both started kissing each other and pulling off their shirts and pants in a frantic yanking.

And then Moshe's cell phone rang. He let it go to voice mail. It rang again and again. At the fourth call, Moshe became alarmed and gestured to Galit with clasped fingers. "A moment, please."

It was Sarah. She was crying. Through Sarah's sobs he heard that she needed to talk to him, right now. Moshe looked at Galit and started stuttering into the phone, trying to find a good excuse, a good explanation, a good reason to say no to her and to return to the issue at hand. Sarah started yelling, "Why don't you want to meet with me? I need to talk with you!"

Galit heard Sarah and started backing away from Moshe.

Then Moshe caved in and yelled, "Okay, I will meet you in a half an hour at Hillel's cafe." When he hung up, Moshe looked guilty.

Galit looked at him suspiciously. "What happened? Who was that?"

Moshe tried to explain that it was his hysterical ex-girlfriend, but Galit grabbed her shirt and pulled it fiercely over her head. Moshe said, "What are you doing? We still have time!"

Galit snarled, "No, you are choosing her over me!" and she then ran out the door.

Moshe stood shirtless and stunned. *This is not fair!* he thought. *I want Galit, not Sarah.* He sat down in his cheap plastic chair and slumped over his kitchen table. "It's not fair," he muttered.

At the coffee shop, Moshe saw Sarah sitting in a dark corner, wedged in like an animal protecting itself from an unknown threat. He pulled out a chair and awkwardly sat across from her.

"*Shalom,*" he said, and she weakly returned the greeting. Her eyelids were red, and she looked disheveled and distracted.

"So what is going on with you?" Moshe asked.

Sarah started to tell him that her boyfriend had left her for a younger woman but quickly broke down in sobs, unable to finish the sentence. Moshe sullenly looked at her for a moment and said, "Why are you telling me this? Are you trying to get back together with me?"

"Yes!" Sarah said, biting her lip and giving him her best doe-eyed look.

Moshe quickly weighed his options. *Galit is probably done with me, and Sarah is now offering me access. What do I have to lose?* he thought. He reached across to grasp her hand, which was cold and clammy. He said gently, "Why don't we go back to my apartment and talk about it some more." He thought, *I am going to score tonight, one way or another.*

chapter 33

RACHEL ATTENDED A DAY-LONG professional conference on sex therapy at Bar Ilan University in Tel Aviv. The psychology department had hosted the conference, inviting speakers from around the world. The conference was a buzz of activity. Rachel met many people whose research she had read. After she had presented a paper during one of the panels, she stepped outside of the room to find a cup of coffee.

She wandered over to a table with coffee dispensers and cups. She recognized a man as one of the speakers on her panel. "Hi! Wonderful presentation, by the way," she said as she stuck out her hand to congratulate him. He just looked down at her hand, stood motionless, and stuttered a curt reply. Then he turned and walked away. Rachel was shocked and stood immobile at the table with an empty cup in her left hand.

"Oh, he is Orthodox. He cannot touch a female non-family member!" a woman said to Rachel as she grabbed a coffee cup. They laughed. "Funny that this happened at a sex therapy conference!" Rachel replied, grinning broadly.

"Welcome to Israel, the land of paradoxes! My name is Sarah, by the way."

"Thanks for enlightening me, Sarah! My name is Rachel."

"I know. I just saw your presentation. It was very good. Want to talk?" she said.

They filled their coffee cups and sought a vacant table.

Rachel asked Sarah, "How did they ever equate shaking hands as a form of social greeting with having sexual intercourse?"

Sarah laughed loudly and slapped the table. "Good one!"

Rachel continued. "If I met an old rabbi with a long stringy beard, yellow teeth, and disarrayed gray hair that needed washing, the last thing I'd want to do is shake his hand and then pull him into a vacant room and have sex with him. That is an adolescent male fantasy."

"I agree, Professor Rachel!" Sarah said gleefully. And they both laughed heartily.

"Instead I'd want to have a long conversation with him about life, about God. After all, that is his role and that is what I'd expect him to give me, not sex."

"Yes, but the male ego believes otherwise." They both laughed again.

Sarah started asking Rachel about her professional job, her interest in the sex therapy field, and how she ended up in Israel. "I am sorry, but I don't want to talk about reasons why I came here," Rachel said quietly.

"No problem. Many people who come to Israel often can't explain what drove them here. It's like an invisible force pushed them here," Sarah said.

Rachel nodded and said, "How about you? Why are you at this conference?"

Sarah explained that she was studying psychology, had heard about this conference, and immediately decided to attend.

"Do you want to become a sex therapist?" Rachel asked.

"I don't know yet. I know I like the topic of sex, but I don't know if I can handle hearing about everyone's problems with sex all day long. I can't even handle my own problems! What kind of therapist would I be?" Sarah said, frowning and looking away.

"May I ask if something happened recently? You look upset," Rachel said gently.

Sarah began to recount the story of her recent ex-boyfriends, including Moshe. She concluded, "I don't know what to think about Moshe! It's been a roller-coaster relationship! I'm so confused!" She drew in a quick breath and bit her lip.

Rachel started consoling Sarah. "I can't be your counselor, because that'd be unethical of me. But I can say a few things as a woman." Sarah nodded and gestured with her hand, inviting Rachel to continue.

Rachel sat back in her chair and said, "I've learned to be more careful about my romantic emotions, because I have learned that the unfolding of a person's true character takes weeks and months, if not years. I might feel attracted to someone I just met, but I don't know who he really is. He might be a jerk, a liar, a depressed guy, an addict, an extreme egoist, or worse—an abuser, a person into satanic rituals, or someone into freaky sex."

Rachel continued, "Some call it testing the guy, others call it building trust. But my approach helped me reduce the extreme emotionality and reactivity I see in many of my female friends. They sleep with a guy after a date or two and then they hyper-analyze them to guess what the man is thinking. All this is from a handful of conversations and dates. It's like they want immediate results and answers. But as therapists, we know that the truth about a person unfolds slowly over time," Rachel said softly.

"But can you really know another person?" Sarah asked.

Rachel chuckled. "That is a profound question. Are people really unknowable? Or do we learn by approximations of the truth? It's a good question indeed. Personally, I view it kind of like calculus. I think that I can have a greater approach to the truth about people over time. It is very hard for people to change even small things about themselves. Eventually, I think you can know who they really are if you observe them closely enough. People can't hide their true characters forever."

Sarah silently looked at Rachel for a moment. Her eyes looked glassy, as if she was about to cry. Then she said, "Thank you so much. That really helps me!"

chapter 34

RACHEL STOOD READING THE signs on the wall in the Tower of King David museum in Jerusalem. Suddenly, she smelled a sweet fragrance that made her imagine a field of purple flowers waving in the wind. She turned around to see a woman wearing a black hijab that was lined with a glittering band of rhinestones. The woman was reading the placard and scribbling in a notebook. The woman muttered something as she looked at her own writing.

Rachel said to her, "It's a lot of information to take in, yes?"

The woman nodded vigorously and replied with a heavy accent, "Oh yes, and I don't agree with all of it! But that's what my paper will be about." She smiled and gestured to her notebook.

Rachel laughed and said, "Yes. What country does not have its own interpretation of history?"

"Ah, you must not be Jewish then?" Fatima asked.

"No, I was raised as a Christian, in America," Rachel replied.

"You are the first American Christian I have met! Do you have time for a coffee?"

"Sure, I am ready now for some caffeine. Too much information to absorb," Rachel said with a wide sweep of her arm, gesturing to the museum room.

"Let's go. *Yella yella*, as they say in Arabic!" Fatima joked.

As they walked to the open-air café at the museum, Fatima

and Rachel started exchanging basic information: where they were born, how big their families were, and what they were doing at the museum. "And do you have a profession? Or are you married?" Fatima asked Rachel, gesturing to Rachel's left hand.

"I was married, and I do have a profession" Rachel told her a little about both aspects of her life.

"You know, here in the Middle East, most women who have a profession do not marry."

"Well, there are many women like that in America," Rachel replied.

"Ah, but the difference is that they have a choice to stay at home or to work, or to do both. I was reading about that." Fatima told Rachel about recently discovering Friedan's book.

"Ah, yes, that book created a lot of feminists!"

"Are you one?" Fatima asked.

"In certain ways, I definitely am. I believe in equality between the sexes. But I'm not rigid and angry about this topic like some feminists are. I still like men!" They both laughed.

Fatima replied, "I do too. But I'm also wary of men in my culture. They seemed to either categorize a woman as an easy prey or a pure one who is preserved for marriage. And in many countries under Muslim law, men can marry four wives. But even with the ability to have multiple women, many men in my culture continue the sexual games and flirtations. I hear this all the time from my Muslim friends. Even right after they married, they watched their husbands continue to flirt with other women! Even on their honeymoon, which should be the height of their passion! This was heartbreaking to my friends. What do they have to look forward to in life? They just hope to have children to love."

Rachel murmured in astonishment. "That sounds like a sexual addiction to me!"

Fatima continued. "I think that many of the men with four wives lack self-control. This makes women powerless in some ways, because they can do nothing to stop these men. And it is hard to get a divorce and survive on your own here. Your parents don't want you back. It's no wonder that they get depressed." Rachel nodded in agreement.

Fatima continued, "Add to this situation the ugly tradition in many Muslim countries of female genital cutting, which often is more like mutilation. This makes the women doubly helpless—they cannot control their men's behaviors and they get no satisfaction from sexual stimulation."

"I've read about this practice. I know it's a cultural ritual, but it makes no sense to me."

"Ah, I'm talking with the right woman! I can tell you my thoughts." Fatima told Rachel about her own experiences. As a young girl, she experienced a less severe form of the practice, thanks to the intervention of her mother, Najib. More than fifty years ago, Najib had been severely injured during the ritual procedure, and she had pain and urinary problems ever since. Najib wanted to protect Fatima from the immense trauma she'd experienced as a child, which had altered her life in a bad way. Fatima was grateful for Najib's insistence that her ritual involved only a slight, shallow scar and not the major surgery that caused some young girls to die from infection and others to experience chronic pain the rest of their lives.

Fatima told Rachel, "As I was growing up, my mother whispered many things to me about women's rights and that a virtuous woman does not need traumatic surgery to reconfigure her genital region as a mark of purity. My mother insisted that it was enough to live properly, to wear the hijab, and to be escorted by a man when in public. And my mother whispered to me when I was becoming a teenager that there are religious people who go to the mosque and say prayers, but then they go home and treat their spouse and kids cruelly. She told me, 'This is hardly a model of love! Don't listen to them! Don't let them control you!'"

Fatima and Rachel talked about how their mothers were

"closet feminists," whispering words of empowerment to their daughters as they cooked dinner for their families and did the laundry and cleaning. "They wanted to break free, but they never tried," Rachel said.

Fatima agreed. "Yes, indeed! And there's a lot that I want to break free from here. One topic that I can't ever talk about at home is suicide bombing. Several of my family members are convinced that it's an important tool in the fight against Israel. But all I see is bloodshed on both sides. I hate suicide bombing! It really should be called homicide bombing! It is a disgrace to Islam."

Rachel turned pale when Fatima mentioned suicide bombing, but she nodded in agreement.

Fatima did not pick up on the change in Rachel, so she continued talking. "I think it is bizarre that these jihadists are trying to act *as* God by taking the lives of other people, even though they claim they are acting *for* God. As if God would ever want destruction of His own creation like that! They claim that their violence will bring them peace in the afterlife. Where'd they get that idea? How does violent killing bring peace? And it is so ironic how the male suicide bombers need the incentive of seventy-five virgins awaiting them. Tell me, if a Muslim man was not permitted seventy-five virgins on earth, then why would it be okay in heaven? They are permitted only four wives on earth." Rachel looked at Fatima with astonishment but said nothing.

Fatima added with a cynical grin, "Anyway, imagine dealing with the mood swings and demands of seventy-five women. How would that be heaven? Virgins get jealous too. As if the women would ever be okay with this setup! They'd fight to be top dog, queen of the lot. It'd be hell to live with all that in-fighting!"

Fatima and Rachel laughed, and Rachel quietly added, "How ironic it would be if a suicide bomber arrives in the next life, expecting to bask in pleasure with dozens of women. But when he shows up, he discovers that, just like on earth, the women are arguing, fighting, and being nasty to each other. There'd be no peace there."

"And that's what those ugly, vicious men deserve!" Fatima proclaimed.

chapter 35

FATIMA ACCEPTED A SCHOLARSHIP to study at University of Oxford in England. Once she had received the offer letter, she had e-mailed them, asking "When can I start?" She found out that she could enter a summer program. So she quickly packed her bags and left within a few months after being accepted. *I won't let my family stop me!* she thought.

The holiday break in December arrived, and she returned for the first visit since starting school. It seemed to her that her family had exponentially grown when she was England. There were children of her relatives everywhere. She brought home modest gifts for all of the children. They looked at their new toys with disappointed faces. After a minute, they had eaten the special candy that she had brought, and they ran out the door with big smiles on their faces. *Note to self: just bring candy for them next time*, she thought with a laugh.

All the women in-laws showered Fatima with affection and attention when she first arrived, fighting for the right to have her visit for dinner. Fatima dreaded the first week, because that was when the rivalry typically manifested itself after guests came into town. That was when the problems began. One sister wanted this, that sister-in-law wanted that, and all wanted to have the first visit. Fatima knew that her choice would set off rumors based on assumptions of favoritism or avoidance.

After she had made the obligatory rounds of dinners at each sibling's apartment, each packed with kids, they stopped fighting over her. She thought that her schedule was once again her own. Fatima just wanted some time alone, away from everyone and their social pressures, their gossip, and their loudness. She just wanted to wander around the Old City of Jerusalem and not think about anything.

Fatima got up before sunrise when she heard the Muslim call to prayer. She threw on her clothes and tried to sneak out the door. That was impossible. A few siblings saw her leaving and invited themselves along for the stroll. The group blossomed with the addition of three younger children. And preparations for the walk turned into an hour of waiting. One child needed to eat, another needed shoes and socks, another needed a new diaper. Then the first needed to use the bathroom, and the second wanted something to eat, and the third wanted to play.

Upon returning from the walk, her three married sisters pounced on Fatima. They all wanted to tell her their latest gossip about people they knew, and then they wanted to tell Fatima everything that they had been doing recently, and then they urgently wanted to complain about their husbands and brothers. Fatima knew that the visiting process could last a few days with each sister. Fatima did not want to hear the stories and complaints, but she sat patiently through the avalanche of words in order to avoid her sisters' condemnation. *If I refuse to talk with them, they will call me selfish,* Fatima thought.

The word *selfish* had a lengthy and painful history for Fatima. In her community, it was the label placed on a woman of child-bearing years who did not have children and who made no efforts to marry. From the time she'd decided to pursue a university degree in England, she had heard the women of her family whispering that word about her. The word made her wince every time she heard it.

It is ironic, Fatima thought, *that I am learning how to think, to write, to teach, but they think these are selfish pursuits for a woman. A woman is supposed to marry, get pregnant as many times as possible, and then raise a large family on the husband's meager income in a small apartment in a noisy, dusty city.* Fatima smiled wryly and wrote in her diary, *It's amazing that the women who call me selfish are the very beings who talk non-stop, all day, to me without once asking about me about my life, my studies, and my friends. Selfish? Who is being selfish?*

One day she decided to confront the women of her family as they sat around Najib's living room having tea. They had once again started asking Fatima about when she was going to marry and have children. Fatima stood up and turned red in the face.

"How selfish is it for me to educate myself and get a job so I do not have to depend on anyone for money, food, and shelter? Is that selfish? Really now?" she heatedly challenged the women, who looked at her with shock. "Isn't it more selfish to depend on someone else when you are a capable adult?" The women started murmuring in response, but nobody said anything.

Fatima continued. "Maybe it is more selfish to create a bunch of hungry little mouths who need your constant attention and care? Maybe it is selfish to create children who need and depend on you for their very lives until they are young adults?" Fatima heard the women gasp and saw the horror on their faces. She stood up straighter and said, "Maybe it is selfish to demand that your family must love you over everyone else in the world? I am sure that there are a lot more kind, funny, supportive, helpful, and intelligent people than me. I don't expect that anyone must love me."

"Fatima, you are being too hard, too intellectual. Children naturally love their parents. And parents naturally think the world of their children," a quiet young lady said from the corner of the room.

"Your academic success is only escapism!" hissed an aunt.

"Yes, and you are trying to run away from life," Najib told Fatima. Her sisters, aunts, cousins, and other assorted women agreed and shouted over each other about how Fatima's interest in academics was useless in the Grand Scheme of Things.

"It won't help you get a man!" one yelled.

"It'll frighten men off and prevent you from getting married and fulfilling your womanly destiny!" another yelled.

Fatima stood awkwardly for a moment and looked at the women. She then firmly said, "I don't think I want to marry and have children." She stepped over the outstretched legs of women sitting on the couch and walked out of the living room. She could hear her mother, Najib, shrieking and yelling that she was about to faint. *Let her faint then,* Fatima thought as she walked out the front door of the apartment into the noisy, humid Jerusalem air.

During the past several years when she'd lived at home, Fatima never asked her parents for money. Instead, she had supplemented her meager allowance with a skimpy paycheck from working at a library. She worked there for three years. She loved her library job and knew on the first day that she started that she was destined to attend a university.

Once she entered university in England, Fatima studied hard. She worked at a part-time job in the Oxford University library. She never asked anyone for money. Once, when she needed immediate help for paying a university bill, her parents wired her money. But she sent them money weekly until their loan was paid off.

When she was visiting during the holiday break, Fatima watched as her younger sisters sauntered up to their father, smiled coyly, and asked him for money, flashing their beautiful dark eyes. This made Fatima cringe. Fatima saw their twisted little smiles, knowing that their father would melt into their wishes. Anger bubbled up under her skin. "I will never grovel in front of a man for money," she swore to herself.

Fatima lay on her bed and listened to the traffic noise outside her window and the family noise beyond her door. She thought about the American TV show that she had just watched and pulled out her diary to write her thoughts down. *It is funny how many women, American or other nationalities, worry so much about being slender. They somehow think that this is the requirement for men to be attracted to or love them. They become highly self-critical about themselves and become oversensitive to the possibility of any remarks about their looks. They don't think about the two billion women in the world who do not have access to gyms, spas, tanning booths, and 'corrective surgical treatments,' or that these billions of women still have husbands and often marry sooner than American women. They have children, so it is obvious that they are having sex. These women, like my married sisters, don't worry about working out or the shape of their body, the tone of their arms, or the size of their bottom or calves. They are too busy carrying or chasing around children and doing the difficult daily labor of household maintenance. Their bodies are naturally sculpted by their lives,* Fatima wrote.

She pulled out some gum, unwrapped a few pieces, popped them her mouth, smiled, and then continued writing. *Many modern women panic when they see slight flabbiness in certain areas of their bodies. They don't think that maybe it's the uptight, self-critical comments and snarky criticisms of others that make them unattractive and push men away. They blame it on their fat and not their joyless life and their obsession with weight, eating, and working out. Their drive toward self-perfection means that they also can't accept others who are imperfect. Plenty of babies have been born to women who have only two sets of clothes and no workout routines. Women in China, Russia, and Africa still have active sex lives, as evidenced by their many babies, even though their bodies and clothing do not reflect the pages of Western-style fashion magazines.*

Fatima paused to lean out of her small bedroom window to catch a glimpse of the reddish hues of the setting sun. She sat down and continued writing. *And these behaviors from the uptight modern woman have the effect of repelling men, because they expect so much and give so little. They believe they should be chased, romanced, and married but only by a select group of worthy men. It's like they are sexual materialists, thinking that the only people who have sex are ones who look like skinny models or Marlboro men. I bet they assume that everyone who is older or has an obvious physical imperfection does not have sex. I bet they think sexuality is an elite process that occurs only when a woman "looks hot" and feels good about herself. But I bet you fifty American dollars that the women who are obsessed about their body weight are less relaxed during sex. I bet they enjoy it less than the women who accept themselves as they are in body, mind, and soul, including their ten extra-pounds and many imperfections.*

Fatima's family seemed to believe that everyone should know each other's business. After her semester of freedom in England, Fatima felt suffocated at home. *Too many people, too much noise, too many demands and chaotic events, too many hurt feelings ... I can't think straight here!* Fatima thought. She craved time alone and sat in her bedroom for hours, reading and writing.

"Ah, she thinks she is too good for us!" the sisters cackled, and they talked about Fatima's hiding in her room and her lack of interest in their conversations.

I just want to have a conversation with my family that does not have the phrase my child *or* my husband *in it*, she wrote in her diary. *These women think that they are so family-focused, but I think they are actually small-minded, ignorant, and selfish in their own ways. Their conversations revolve around everything that they are doing and thinking and experiencing and nothing about what people outside of their family circle are doing or thinking or experiencing—unless, of course, it involves juicy gossip. They only think about dresses, makeup, cooking, and marriage choices. But I knew there was no turning back for me once I dove into the world of ideas and learning. I am expanded by reading and studying. My motto is that you grow in proportion to your knowledge. And I want to become wise and mature.*

As Fatima lay on her bed, memories of family life of her early years flooded her with feelings of warmth and happiness. She wrote about some of those memories in her diary. And then she added, *But when I visit them, all I see around me is ugliness, harshness, and criticism. How can my memories and the realities be so different? How can my family, which I love dearly, be so closed-minded, arrogant, and self-centered?*

She thought about her family rituals, which were based on religious traditions. *Some of these practices have a very bitter taste to them,* she wrote. *My mother would spend all day cooking and preparing a special meal for her family and friends, while yelling sharply at everyone within view. I used to hate that. The day of religious celebration was filled with tension, argument, and anger. Why practice these traditions if they stress you out so much?* she wrote.

Fatima put her diary down and gazed out of the window into the narrow streets. *I am suffocating here!* she thought. She imagined running out into the fresh but dusty air of the desert, where there were no human pressures to live or act a certain way. *I want my freedom back!* she thought. She pictured the quiet halls of Oxford, where studying was not viewed as selfish but as a ticket to higher levels of thinking and being. *In the world of ideas, there is freedom,* she thought, *unlike this oppressive home life, where any views that conflict with my family or community are viewed as wrong and evil. So this is who I am. I am a blasphemous feminist!* She smiled to herself as she turned out the light.

chapter 36

RACHEL LOOKED AT HER plane ticket. *Five days before I go home. What else should I do?* She thought about calling her friends, but she just sat in her chair and stared out of the window. She did not want to read anything or listen to the radio. An image of Mr. Hit-and-Run entered her mind. *I wonder what he really thinks about me?* His image lingered in her mind. *I hope I see him soon!* she thought. *But what the hell am I thinking? He is married!* She briefly imagined him touching, kissing, and having sex with his wife. The thought made her nauseous.

Rachel looked at the clock. She looked at her cell phone. She looked at the TV. *What should I do tonight? Maybe I should go out to a bar to dance and listen to music?* She stretched out in her chair. *What's the use? I could have sex with whomever I wanted to right now, if I really wanted to. I am free. But I don't want to. I only want him, Mr. Unavailable. Mr. Married. Mr. Hit-and-Run. I think I need psychological help,* she thought.

Rachel mentally reviewed her multiple failures in love in the past decades. She often fell in love with a guy who either was chasing somebody else, or who paid attention to her briefly and then hit the road. *I really did not like any of those guys in the end, anyway. Not much substance to them,* she thought.

Rachel thought of a quote written by King Solomon in his Proverbs, which she'd read earlier that day: A person who courts sin, marries trouble. She thought, *I must stop thinking about Mr. Hit-and-Run. He's married. I have lost my objectivity over him,* she thought. *That's a sign of big-time infatuation! And maybe some mental health issues, too. I am in trouble!*

An image of Rachel's parents crossed her mind. She felt jealous about their assuredness and certainty about life. *They know what they will do tomorrow, who will fix dinner, who will take out the trash, who will pay the bills. But me, I'm not sure about anything since my divorce, since my sons died and my daughter drifted into drug and alcohol addiction. The only thing I can be sure of is that my heart and lungs are working right now. I don't know if my heart will continue to beat and my lungs will continue to breathe tomorrow. Who can predict the future?*

Rachel's parents had been married for more than forty-five years. She wondered why they never divorced, because they were constantly arguing. Her mother seemed bitter and angry all the time, and her father seemed sullen and bossy. When Rachel visited her parents, she felt like she was caught in an emotional web. They both vied for her attention and compliments, like little kids. Both tried to outdo the other with helpfulness. She did not like being in this kind of emotional triangle with her parents.

All I wanted was for them to be honest with themselves and each other about the state of their relationship and their discontent with each other. Neither likes the thought of change or the burden of the responsibility for initiating a change. Why can't they be honest with themselves? she thought. *The evidence of their unhappiness is clear for all the family to see—the bickering, arguing, always taking the opposite point of view. Their unhappiness shows in their faces. They look drained of life and joy. Is this emotional sparring supposed to be a good marriage? I think refusing to leave a bad marriage is a form of emotional slavery!*

One day about twenty years before, Rachel had encouraged

her mother to get a divorce. But her mother snapped back, saying, "I cannot do that! After all, what would the family do about Thanksgiving?" This reply left Rachel stunned. She thought to herself, *But now I understand. Many people use family as the organizing force for meaning in their lives. And that is okay. This is beneficial to many kids. But people can also hide behind families. The marriage becomes all about the kids. These kinds of parents tend to let their kids run the show. And many of them let the kids do all the talking so that they don't have to intelligently communicate with their spouse at the dinner table.*

Rachel pictured the unhappy faces of her parents and thought, *They will do what they want, but that life is not for me. I won't stay with a man I don't trust or like just for the sake of the kids.* At that thought, images of her two sons as infants flashed in her mind. She remembered them as adorable babies, smiling their toothless grins, cooing with global pleasure over life, and then as adolescents involved in endless sports games, homework, and activities. She sighed heavily.

As a therapist, Rachel talked with countless spouses who had discovered the affairs of their partners yet did not leave. At first, she was curious how that could be. She started asking these clients, "What prevents you from leaving?" She started seeing a pattern. Their main fear was living alone. Even if they could afford a divorce and could get their own place, they would not do it because they were afraid of loneliness and embarrassed by the label of being alone. Rachel noticed that these same people liked to use the royal *we* term with pride. She thought, *They think the most important thing is to never be alone! That's intolerably embarrassing!* We *at all costs.* We *or die!*

chapter 37

THE DAY WAS GRAY and drizzly. *Another Shabbat with all the stores closed,* Moshe thought. *What can I do today?* He thought about Sarah and their last meeting. He did not get what he wanted that night from either Sarah or Galit. Sarah had talked to him for hours and then finally told him goodnight. She did not return any of his daily calls that whole next week. *Let me try to mend things with Galit,* he thought and grabbed his cell phone.

"Galit? Hello, it is Moshe. Wait, don't hang up. Let's have another coffee. I really want to talk with you!" She agreed to meet him that evening, after stores reopened at the end of the Sabbath.

A few hours later, they sat at a coffee house near Galit's house.

"How's little Anat?" Moshe asked.

"She's the best! My friend Netti is watching her," Galit said, and she hurriedly sipped her coffee. They started talking about their jobs, the people they knew, and Israeli politics.

"What do you do with Anat while you work?" Moshe asked, curious how Galit could handle being a manager of a clothing store and a single mother.

"Oh, Netti takes care of her."

"How can you afford all this babysitting?" Moshe asked with surprise.

Galit hesitated, and said "Oh, you know. It works out okay." She quickly sipped her coffee and asked Moshe about his thoughts on the recent political battle going on in the Knesset.

After talking for an hour, Moshe asked Galit about her dreams for the future and whether she planned to marry and have more children.

"No, no. I don't want to marry. I don't need more complications. Life is hard enough already. "

Moshe looked at her for a moment and said, "Why? You are such a beautiful woman! What about Anat? Doesn't she need a father?"

Galit looked flustered and quickly picked up her cell phone. "Thanks for reminding me. Excuse me. I better call to check on Anat." She stood and walked to the door of the coffee shop while she called Netti. She stood by the door, looking through it and watching the street activities as she talked on the phone.

A man walking by on the sidewalk suddenly stopped. He looked shocked and quickly turned to open the door to the cafe. He said "Galit, my love, what are you doing here?" as he started to hug and kiss her on the lips.

She stepped back out of his embrace. "Amos! I … I …. One moment, I was calling about Galit. Let me get off the phone."

"Ah, let me talk to my mother." He grabbed the cell phone out of Galit's hand as he draped his arm around Galit and said, "Hi, Mom! How's my daughter?"

Moshe heard every word. He stood up and walked up to Galit. "Oh, so this is the father? And you two are together?" he asked.

Amos nodded vigorously. "And who are you?"

"I was her date!" Moshe hissed. "But I am out of here. Good-bye, Galit. Don't call me," Moshe said, brushing past Amos and slamming the door on his way out.

"You're seeing him? What's this?" Amos yelled at Galit.

"Please. Shhh. No. We were just talking. He called me!" Galit said defensively.

"Oh. You're dating other men, are you? I thought so. You are a liar. It's over between us, Galit. I am done with you!" Amos yelled as he slammed the door after exiting the coffee shop.

Galit opened the door and yelled, "Wait! Amos! What about Anat?"

Amos turned around and said, "She's still my daughter. At least I think she is. I'll be requesting a paternity test though. I will go get my stuff and be done with this nightmare!" Amos ran down the street.

Galit stood at the door. She looked into her cell phone and then around at the people in the coffee shop watching her. "He's crazy. He doesn't know what he is talking about," she said. People looked down at their coffee or at their cell phones. Galit slid out the door and hurried down the street.

Amos stormed into their apartment and greeted his mother, Netti, and Anat, who were playing with toys on the floor. "What happened? What's wrong, my love?" she said to Amos. "Tell me! Did someone die? What happened?"

"I don't want to talk about." He grabbed his old army duffel bag and started shoving clothes into it.

"Please tell me. You are upsetting Anat!" Netti said. Anat started crying, and Netti picked her up. "Talk to me, Amos, please."

Amos told her what had just happened and that he'd caught Galit with another man, who claimed to be her date.

"I never trusted her," she said to Amos. "Let me help you. You can stay with me as you sort things out. I will pack some toys and clothes for Anat." They put Anat in front of the TV and started packing.

chapter 38

SOLOMON OPENED HIS EYES and sat up suddenly. "Today is the day the queen of Sheba arrives!" He started to jump from his bed, but he looked back and then rolled under the covers. There he collided with his lover. He shook her until she woke up. He laughed and kissed her, and they enjoyed a few moments of intimacy. He got out of bed, kneeled quickly before his altars to Molech and Ashtoret, said a few prayers of thanks, and then turned back to look at the woman on his bed, who nodded at him approvingly.

Solomon ebulliently ran out of his chambers, and his advisors quickly followed him. They told him that the queen of Sheba's camels could be seen on the horizon, which meant that she should arrive before nightfall. He shouted directions to everyone he ran into. Energy radiated from Solomon's face.

The queen of Sheba arrived in a magnificent caravan full of colors and glinting gold ornaments. She was hidden behind a curtain, so Solomon could not see her. She sent a message of lengthy greetings and asked him to excuse her until the next morning. Solomon ran around his palace with a fervor and excitement that made his women laugh. "Like a little boy!" they murmured to themselves.

Solomon made sure that the whole caravan was taken care of that evening—from the servants, guards, and advisors to the camels and donkeys. The sounds of laughter and music echoed through Jerusalem. Solomon ate his dinner quickly and then ran around to various groups, talking with them, making sure they had food and water and that they were comfortable. He was a terrific host. He could not sleep that night because of the excitement in the air and the upcoming meeting, for which he had waited many years.

Solomon sprang up with the rising of the sun and ran to the quarters where the queen of Sheba was sleeping. "Is the queen okay? Is she rested? Does she need something?"

Her advisors smiled and bowed to Solomon, saying, "You have been a most gracious host. She will meet you in your court very soon."

Solomon paced like a trapped lion as he waited and waited. Finally, trumpets sounded. It seemed the whole city ran to the streets to watch the regal procession of the queen of Sheba to Solomon's court. The queen had black hair and kohl-lined eyes. She looked solemn, like a pharaoh. She stepped before Solomon, bowed, and then looked up and smiled widely, meeting Solomon's gaze. "I finally meet the wisest man in the world," she said.

"Only God is wise," Solomon replied. "I am still learning." The people gathered in the chambers chuckled at this comment. "Please, my queen, sit beside me," Solomon said as he gestured to her to sit on beside him on his huge ivory throne.

"It is my honor to sit by you," she said. "I have read your many insightful sayings. You instruct your people well. But tell me, why do you say 'All is dust'? This does not look like dust to me," she said, gesturing around his luxurious court and toward the temple. People in the court laughed and murmured among themselves.

"It is dusty when you ride through the desert to Jerusalem," Solomon replied with a smile.

"The king has a sense of humor!" the queen of Sheba responded.

"Only when you realize that all is dust, that all will disappear with time, can you make light of what we have and do," King Solomon answered.

"It looks like your magnificent temple to your God will not disappear any time soon," she said.

"Only God knows a person's time of birth and place of death, of the change of the seasons, the creation and destruction of kingdoms, and the rise and fall of kings and queens," Solomon said, looking right into the eyes of the queen of Sheba.

"You speak the truth, my king. And tell me this—who knows the heart of man?" she asked.

"Often it is not himself who knows," Solomon replied with a smile.

A person in the chamber yelled, "But his woman knows!" The chamber erupted in laughter.

"I have heard of your many wives. This must mean that many women know your heart?" the queen asked, returning her smile.

"You asked about the heart of man, not the heart of a king. A king must not rule with his heart, because if he does, his kingdom will fall. He must rule with justice and wisdom," King Solomon replied stately.

"So no woman rules your heart?" she said, continuing to smile.

"Not *one*," Solomon replied, firmly emphasizing the second word. The chamber exploded with laughter. "Women are a gift, and they enrich my days," he continued. "As I believe that you also will do during your visit."

"Indeed, I will, King Solomon. Starting from this moment," the queen of Sheba said, and then she clapped her hands. Her servants started bringing in beautiful gifts and bags of fragrant spices. Women dressed in colorful northern African styles brought in cups, vases, and ornaments made of gold. The train of gifts lasted for two hours and included four and half tons of gold, much of which was hammered into glistening, intricate objects.

chapter 39

FATIMA'S FORMER LOVER CONTACTED her by e-mail about six months after she stopped speaking with him. "I love you, Fatima. Come back to Palestine and be with me." He mentioned some of the sexual encounters that they had had and how he missed that. Fatima was furious. She refused to e-mail him back, thinking, *If you are not going through a divorce, then I am not going to talk about sex with you.* She shut the computer off quickly and turned away from it in disgust.

She grabbed her diary to write down her thoughts. *What about my pleasure? When did you ever think about that? You assumed that just being with you gave me pleasure. Egoist! You were always out of my reach because you are married. But you kept stroking my hopes and talking about "maybe someday." You left me destabilized and dissatisfied. Why live like that? No more secret love. You were just a fantasy. The reality is that you are an immoral, manipulative liar and have a very hard heart. Who would want that? Your wife can have you!* she wrote angrily.

I was a fool to believe that you'd change. People don't like to change. But now I know. I am the one who must change! she wrote. She underlined the last sentence twice. *It was only my fantasy, though it was a very delicious one. It just was a fantasy that you would divorce for me. You did not need to divorce because you already had me. You were safe in your little family cocoon. I had no boundaries with you, but now I am going to build a brick wall.*

I want a man who is attracted by me and attractive to me, instead just attracted to me, she wrote on a new page under the title, MY FUTURE. Fatima strode across the cramped room, pulled out her suitcase, and started packing for her trip at the end of the school year. *How many of us live our lives unconsciously?* she thought.

Fatima returned to Jerusalem to visit her family during the height of the summer heat. She dreaded the visit and felt very awkward around her gossiping sisters, nosey mother, and male family members, who seemed uninterested in anything remotely connected to her new life except English rugby teams.

Oppression returns to my life, Fatima thought. After the second day home, she thought, *I have to get out of here!* She grabbed her purse and mumbled an excuse to her mother, who was right in the middle of feeding Fatima's younger siblings. "I'll be back in a few hours!" she yelled over her shoulder, gesturing to her cell to indicate that she could be contacted in an emergency, such as her mother trying to decide what to cook for dinner.

Fatima ran down the uneven surface of the street. *Where can I go to escape them?* She thought about her old friends and then pictured the cramped apartments that they now lived in, with children peeping out from every corner. *No, I can't call them.*

She ran down the narrow Jerusalem streets until she was thirsty and out of breath. She looked up and saw a sign for Hebrew University. *I'll go there for a soda and then to the library.* She walked up to security and let them scan her body with a security wand and put her purse through the x-ray machine. They eyed her suspiciously when she said that she did not have a student identification card. "But I go to Oxford University. See. Here is my student ID."

Several guards looked at her ID and talked among themselves. They asked her to step out of the search line. They spoke into their radios and then to each other for several minutes. Fatima started getting impatient but said nothing.

Suddenly she heard, "Hey, I remember you!" Fatima looked around and saw Moshe. "Oh, yes. We talked months ago at a coffee shop," she said, smiling faintly.

"I do remember you." Moshe turned to the guards and told them in Hebrew, "She's okay. She was reading *Kosher Sex* when I met her." They laughed heartedly and then repeated what Moshe said into the radios. The radios erupted in a chatter of Hebrew. They handed Fatima her purse and waved her on, still laughing and talking into their radios.

"What did you say to them?" she asked Moshe.

"Keep walking on. It's nothing. Just a joke. I told them I knew you. Where are you going?" he said.

"I need a Coca-Cola!" she said, gesturing to her throat and sticking her tongue out to signal thirst. But the noise that she made sounded like a wounded animal.

"Let's get you a drink!" Moshe took her by the elbow and led her to the cafeteria. They added a plate of salad, hummus, pickles, and pita bread to the soda purchase. Moshe asked about her studies at Oxford, and Fatima enthusiastically told him about her many courses, readings, and discoveries. Moshe told her about his own studies at Hebrew University and his plan to specialize in Middle Eastern politics.

"Oh, really? So you are going to tell me why I am wrong?" Fatima challenged him.

Moshe responded with a smile and said, "No, I will never do that" in Arabic.

Fatima looked delighted. "Oh, have you become fluent in Arabic since I last met you?" she asked.

"No, I have been studying it for years. I was just embarrassed to speak it in front of you," he said with a smile.

"Ah, do I scare you so much? Or does my feminism scare you?" she said.

"It might have a few years ago. But I've grown up since then," Moshe answered, frowning slightly. He looked at his hands and started telling Fatima the story of his engagement to Sarah and how it ended. Then he told her how he met Galit and how it ended by meeting her boyfriend.

"Wow! You've had a rough time recently. I don't understand why people are so impulsive and greedy when it comes to sex," Fatima said, smiling slightly. "I mean, they jump from partner to partner and then complain about the partner they do have. Never satisfied with what, or whom, they have. I'd be happy with one good man that I can trust!" she said emphatically.

"Oh, the feminist likes men, then!" Moshe joked.

"I'll love the right man with all of my heart!" she responded gleefully.

"Really? So do I have a chance?" Moshe said quietly, smiling mysteriously.

Fatima returned his gaze and smiled broadly. "Yes, you do. So—has this become a date?"

"Yes, as of this moment, it has. To us!" Moshe exclaimed in Arabic, and he raised his soda in the air as a toast.

Fatima clinked her bottle of soda with his and responded in Hebrew, "To us!" Then she added, "To life!" in Hebrew, smiling broadly.

chapter 40

ON AN IMPULSE, SARAH pulled out the piece of paper with Rachel's phone number in Israel and called to ask if they could meet one last time before Rachel returned home.

"Sure, I'd be happy to. I was hoping that you'd call me! I enjoyed talking to you at the conference," Rachel said. And they agreed to meet for coffee that evening in Tel Aviv at an outdoor café overlooking the Mediterranean Sea.

"What a beautiful night!" Rachel exclaimed as they sat on the canvas furniture.

"Yes, it is. But I wish I could feel the beauty of the night," Sarah replied.

"What's wrong?" Rachel asked gently.

Sarah told her about Moshe calling her in a fury to tell her about how Galit had lied to him about being single before her boyfriend walked in.

"I didn't say anything to Moshe after he told me the story. I just hung up my phone and turned it off. I knew that he'd keep calling me back."

"Maybe he still loves you?" Rachel asked.

"Yeah, maybe. I know I hurt him, but I don't want to be around him anymore. He has issues. For example, he likes pornography a little too much!"

"Oh, sorry to hear that. How does that make you feel?" Rachel asked.

"I was always willing to please him however he wanted me to. So I don't understand why he needed to watch sex on a screen. Isn't the real thing with me good enough? Why couldn't he just use his imagination if he needed to think about another woman? I think he is a voyeur and he needs psychological help!" Sarah said with a frown, and she looked down at her hands.

"I know this is a big problem nowadays. This is an issue for many of the couples I see in my practice. I don't think it's the core issue, though, but a manifestation of deeper problems."

"Like what?" Sarah asked.

"Of unfulfilled lives. If you look closely, you'll see that these kinds of guys are dissatisfied with most everything in their lives — their jobs, their paycheck, where they live, what they drive, their friends or their lack of close friends."

"Tell me more," Sarah implored.

Rachel continued, "Those guys are often restless. You know, one problem with men who watch pornography a lot or go to strip bars and visit prostitutes is that they have a high stimulus threshold. They get bored easily, so they keep changing their sex partners, thinking that will make a difference. But the sex act is the pretty much the same no matter what her name is. Sure, there are different positions. But sex is really not that complicated. Get aroused, build to a crescendo, and then release. It's humans who make it complicated."

Sarah nodded in agreement and gestured for Rachel to keep talking. "Perceptions of sexuality can get complicated. Take, for example, men who go to prostitutes. What kind of man gets aroused by a woman who does not really like him and actually thinks he is disgusting? These guys don't pick up on the hatred that most women in the sex industry feel for their clients. But strippers and prostitutes encourage the men's delusions that they are desirable even with their fat stomachs, greasy hair, and smelly underarms. After all, there's a paycheck on the line. Prostitutes are great actresses. That's how they keep business going. So they encourage the men to have the delusion that they want him as a person, instead of his money. These men are obviously being played for their money, but they are clueless, except maybe for a small voice inside telling them that this is a lie. But of course, they drown out that voice by drinking or drugging it away. And many of these men don't care what the women they are sexing think. That's what it means to be a sex object. It is not about you as a person, but how much you can arouse and satisfy them."

Sarah replied, "Wow, that sounds a lot like Moshe! He is high-strung and restless, for sure. It didn't feel like we really connected psychologically, just by sex. He really didn't care what I thought, just whether I gave him sex and attention. I wanted to get married, so I said yes to him when he asked me to marry him. But now I look back, and I think, *Ewww. He's weird!*" Sarah said, scrunching up her face.

Rachel nodded and continued, "I think there are many parallels between heavy pornography use and going to prostitutes. Sex with a prostitute is like masturbating inside a woman for a fee. Pornography is sexual stimulation for the purpose of masturbation. So both are ways to easy sex, with none of the challenges of pleasing a partner. But of course, actively seeking prostitutes is different from passively sitting at home watching a pornographic video. Pornography makes sex an observer sport, while prostitution involves a pseudo-relationship. The man pays money for someone to pretend to like him and to be excited by his sexual parts. It's a more serious psychological problem because he denies that he is seeking a relationship. He claims that he sees prostitutes because there are no ties, no emotional bonds. But why doesn't he masturbate and get sexual release at his own home if he doesn't need another person?" Rachel asked, looking at the reflection of the moon on the sea.

Sarah added, "I wonder whether these men ever thought that the woman in front of them was someone's daughter. Would such men ever let their own daughters be in such a situation? I think not. So where is their compassion? I want to say to them, 'Can you see your daughter lying there, experiencing the same thing?'"

Rachel responded, "You learn a lot about human nature after working with clients. But what I will never understand are the men who visit prostitutes, or who even pick up women at bars, and don't use a condom during sex. It's like they think they're invincible, that they never will get a disease. How stupid! From a psychotherapeutic perspective, either they have a death wish or subconsciously they need to punish themselves for this behavior. But maybe they never paid attention in their basic biology classes in high school and believe that if a prostitute looks and smells clean, she is clean, biologically speaking. They can't imagine that life can change in an instance—one quick exposure to HIV and that's it. It is like biological Russian roulette."

Sarah vigorously nodded her head and said, "Yes, I know several people who have HIV. All of them were pretty arrogant and thought that they could do whatever the hell they wanted to, sexually speaking. One was an ex-boyfriend."

"Oh my! That's not good. Some people are only stimulated by sneaky sex. Sneakiness and breaking the rules kick up their adrenaline." Rachel paused to look at how Sarah was reacting to what she said.

Sarah nodded and said, "Well, I have been interested in writing my thesis on men who go to strip clubs. They pay to be teased, and I find the dynamic fascinating. There are clear rules to the game—no touching allowed. But voyeurism is fully promoted there. I want to research how these men actually interact with real women. I suspect that many of these men, in fact, have low self-confidence and that they haven't been successful in approaching and seducing women. How do they react when they approach a real woman for sex and get rejected? Does he blow up and swear at the woman? Does he call her a tease? Does he limp back to the strip-club world, where he thinks he can control women by paying them to bare all in front of him?"

"Good questions! That is the start of good research!" Rachel exclaimed. "And the sex therapy field needs more careful, thoughtful researchers like you! There is a lot of suffering out there. For most people, sex is the most intimate form of communication with another person. We need to better understand the dynamics, so as to help more people."

"Thanks! You inspire me to move forward in my studies!" Sarah replied.

"Well, the field is replete with many different research topics. Women also have vast reservoirs of ego issues. It seems like many women either flaunt what they have or are highly critical of what they have and want what someone else has. Me included!" Rachel laughed, and Sarah joined her in laughter.

Rachel continued, "And sex therapy is often closely tied with marital therapy. Marriage is a prime breeding ground for psychological issues affecting sex interactions, especially when love triangles are created. Some people seem to create triangles everywhere—they put their kid in the triangle with their spouse, or they find a lover outside their marriage. But it seems to me that the average Joe Husband often gets in trouble for what he doesn't do for his wife, versus what he does. My female clients tell me that the most hurtful thing is not their husbands' viewing pornography but what their husbands are not doing. These guys are not showering their wives with affection and attention. The average Joe Husband doesn't get that this is what melts women's hearts and inspires them to please their spouse. Most women respond to the fire of the man they love. They'll let their guard down and forget themselves, lost in the beauty of being with the man they love. They'll do almost anything to please a man that they love. So why wouldn't a man try to excite such passions in a woman? The answers are right in front of these guys. They give up too easily!"

"You are right on target about that! And this is true even with boyfriends!" Sarah said emphatically.

Rachel exclaimed, "I can't say this to my clients, but I think that married men who go to prostitutes or have an affair are cowards! They are too afraid of telling their wives to crank up sex so they don't suffer. And they are too afraid of even asking for a divorce so they can legally find another woman to have sex with. Maybe they claim that they don't need rules, that rules are for children. But the subtle thing here is that they stay married. Isn't that following the rules? And the wife may even collude with him if she suspects or outright knows that he's seeing another woman or has a prostitute habit. I have seen it many times before with wives of adulterers. The wife may remain quiet so as to not to rock the family boat. After all, his leaving may cause huge stress and mean that she'll have to work to pay her own bills, care for her children by herself, and have to eat dinner and go on vacation alone. Both spouses remain silent and afraid of speaking the truth about their relationship. But the spouses dislike each other and no longer want to have sex together. So the tension grows and grows."

"Yes, I've seen that in many couples. They're so angry around each other, but they are supposed to be in a beautiful relationship. I don't know why they don't divorce, except for religious or family reasons," Sarah said.

Rachel replied, "I know how difficult it is for people to change. Couples come to me, blaming each other for all sorts of large and small problems, pointing their fingers in anger, even in hate. There was a moment when I realized how tense I became during these sessions. So I decided to restrict my schedule to one unhappy couple per day, even if that meant I'd earn less money. I started to see more unhappy teenagers, because I found that I could relate to their angst. They were often searing in their honesty and sometimes quite profound. But the couples who really dislike each other but won't divorce, even if they are ready to kill each other, really bother me and get under my skin. It seems like some of them keep seeking guidance from a variety of therapists, counselors, psychologists, social workers, psychiatrists, and clergy--but they never do anything to change their situation. They just seek help to convince someone else how they have been wronged! They seek attention, not change."

"Wow, sounds like being a therapist is difficult," Sarah said, leaning forward.

Rachel smiled and said, "Sometimes it is. But not always. Often it becomes clear eventually that one partner could do a whole lot more to nurture the relationship. And the other partner is doing all the work to keep the relationship alive. And many men really miss out on the simple fact of how sexual the average girl could be with the right man and circumstances. If her man does not try to give her some positive feedback, some confidence boosters, she will wallow in the lack of confidence most of us are plagued with. It's only when a woman trusts a man that her floodgates of desire truly open wide and she will achieve lots of sexual pleasure. But men don't understand that those gates close very quickly at the first sign of criticism or cheating. She'll shut down. So the answer is right there! Encourage and support your lover and she'll respond with enthusiasm!"

"This view sounds like the sexual elixir!" Sarah said.

"Yes, indeed. Maybe I should market it!" Rachel laughed.

"Well, Sarah, I'm getting old, so I'll have to go back to my hotel soon," Rachel said laughingly.

"That's totally okay. But can you give me some advice before you leave?" Sarah asked.

"Sure. What are you wondering about?" Rachel replied.

"How do I know which guy to date and marry? Or should I ever get married?" Sarah said gently.

"Do you want to marry?" Rachel asked, looking at her directly with a smile.

"Yes, I think so. It has always been a dream, a goal, of mine." Sarah said, a little guiltily.

"Everyone makes her own choice. Some never marry. But I personally think marriage is the best way," Rachel responded.

"Even though you divorced?" Sarah said in a surprised voice.

Rachel smiled and shrugged, replying "Yes. I believe in marriage, but I have learned that getting married doesn't make a man, or a woman, faithful. It may reflect their faith in the relationship as a whole, but being faithful is a daily process. Some veer off, even if they had every intention to go straight down the fidelity path. What I have learned from my clients' and my own experiences is that we all need to screen the men we date for sexual self-control. People in the modern-day world do not think about the consequences of marrying a man with little self-control. They expect a man to have self-control during the first few dates, but after that, if he doesn't start making sexual advances pretty quickly, they start to think something is wrong with the man. The media and entertainment industries heavily reinforce this idea. And many men, of course, hope that the woman they date exhibits no sexual self-control with them personally, but they want her to have self-control when she is near other men." Rachel paused to see if Sarah wanted her to keep talking.

"Please, tell me more!" Sarah said, gesturing with a wave.

Rachel continued, "Well, women often want the man to be emotionally addicted to them and to worship them alone. So they encourage their man's sexual needs and desires very soon in the relationship. They are afraid of testing whether this man has self-control. They are afraid if they say 'no, not now' too much, the man will leave for bubblier sexual waters. So they never really get a sense of the man's self-control in sexual matters. As a result, they have to resort to close monitoring of the man, because they don't know if the man has self-control when they aren't around. I made this mistake also. But now I know that self-control is key, because it affects other matters, like eating, finances, gambling, alcohol, and drugs. Both genders need to realize that sexual self-control means that a person can be sexual when it's right and stop sexuality when it is not the right person, place, or time. This is much different from thinking that sex will never happen. Rather, it's about having your sexual impulses under control. If it's not, then you probably have a sex addict on your hands. And that is not a pretty picture in any universe!" Rachel exclaimed.

"I hear you. Moshe was like that. And he was blind to himself," Sarah said with a sigh.

Rachel responded, "Yes. It's tricky business to figure this out. Sex is usually fun at first and often is spontaneous and passionate. But then you may see his lack of self-control revealed in constant spending on sporting gear and electronics when he can't afford them, or use of alcohol to the extreme, viewing pornography every day, or, in the worst case, having affairs. We easily assume that an intelligent man with good social skills has self-control. But such men can also use their skills to seduce and betray their lovers. We can be blinded by the smooth-talking, educated man. And we fall for the easy fix, thinking that once we marry, all our problems will be solved. So we overlook the shy, nerdy guys who do not quite have the confidence to ask a woman on a date. Give me a man who might have a little trouble verbalizing his love but who is faithful and dedicated. That is the man I want to marry!" Rachel proclaimed, gesturing with her fist in the air like a battle charge.

Sarah laughed and said, "Wow! Terrific thoughts! Anything else you want to tell me?"

Rachel rubbed her neck and said, "Yes, one last thing and then I will go home. I've learned over many years that women usually get the short end of the deal if they agree to live with a man without marrying him. What they typically get is a man who has trouble making decisions and commitments. They also get a man who requires that his woman gives up all sense of morality and appropriateness. It is his sexual needs or the highway. Of course, there are many liberal, modern women who do not give morality a second thought and dive into any living-together condition. They claim that they need to 'test out the relationship.' But what it often means is that they are too impatient to wait for answers. The man doesn't mind because he gets a free housekeeper, bed companion, and cook. Why would he protest? And why would he want to marry when he has the full deal? He just keeps saying to the woman, 'No promises, no guarantees, no commitments, but give me your sex.'"

Sarah gestured with her hand for Rachel to keep talking.

Rachel sighed and said, "Women used to think about morality, or at least their reputation, and men used to honor them. Now a woman is called uptight or a prude if she waits to have sex until she is married. Many women fear that label, so they run into the arms of any man who looks half-decent, somewhat trustworthy, and has a job. The most important thing to them is to have a man and not be alone!" Rachel exclaimed.

"And what happens to these kinds of women in the end?" Sarah asked, looking expectantly at Rachel.

Rachel replied, "Okay. So let's fast-forward a decade or two later. The woman feels incredibly isolated in her marriage—the marriage that she ran into to protect herself from loneliness. He has drifted into his addictions and away from her. And now she feels stuck, angry, and helpless. She has what she thought she wanted, and technically she is not alone, because she has a husband. But she is deeply lonely. She had a grab-what-you-can and get-someone-so-you-are-not-alone kind of sexuality, so she didn't carefully think about the character of the man she was marrying. So my advice to you, as a friend, is to make sure you find a moral man, or you may end up in a bad place!" Rachel said wistfully. She gently squeezed Sarah's arm.

Sarah smiled back and nodded slowly and thoughtfully.

chapter 41

IN THE MIDDLE OF a clear and cold night, Solomon sat up in his bed, screamed loudly, but then fell silent. He stared ahead of him, into the darkness of his room. His lover mumbled a question, and Solomon quieted her with a hand on her naked back. He got out of his bed and walked back and forth.

Solomon felt a heavy sense of foreboding. He did not know why or what was bothering him. He saw no picture, heard no words. He had never experienced this kind of dread before. He called for his guards and told them to bring the seer to him immediately. The seer was known for being able to glimpse a person's soul and provide wisdom to help the person.

Solomon restlessly walked around the courtyard, up and down, up and down, until the guards returned with the seer. She was gracious to him, although sleep still dwelled in her eyes. They sat down where Solomon held court during the day. Solomon described what happened to him and said he could still feel the force, the presence that awoke him. The seer nodded and asked him for more details.

When Solomon finished telling everything, the seer stood up and said, "God is trying to communicate with you." She spun around and walked to the corner of the room. She covered her head with a veil, closed her eyes, and chanted prayers quietly while she rocked back and forth. Minutes passed. Solomon sat waiting on his ivory throne. Finally, the seer opened her eyes, and said, "My king."

"Yes, please speak." He stood up and walked to her. "Please tell me whatever you need to say. I will not hurt you for what you tell me. Tell me the truth."

She nodded and said, "I fear that this is a warning to you. You must prepare for an attack against your kingdom. I do not know who will attack you or from which direction the attack will come. But this is a warning for you to be ready," she said somberly.

"Is there anything else? Please tell me. I won't harm you, no matter what you tell me!" King Solomon pressed.

"Yes, King Solomon. I see the temple falling down. Please understand that we cannot know the time of the event. It may be tomorrow, or it could be in a few years. Or it could happen when you are an old man. The warning was sent to help you."

"Can you tell me anything more?" he worriedly asked.

"Yes, my king. This will happen because you marry foreign wives."

Solomon stood still and did not say anything for a moment.

"I will stop then," he said. He turned and walked up to her. "Thank you. You are a blessed one." He attempted to place several gold coins in her hand, which she refused, bowing her head. He dropped the coins in her lap and turned to run out of the room, telling his guards to wake his chiefs of staff. They had to prepare for war.

chapter 42

HALFWAY THROUGH HER STUDIES, Fatima accepted a job in England's Coventry School because her scholarship money and library job turned out to be insufficient for covering all of her living expenses. She would teach high school girls full-time during the day and go to classes in the evening.

Her new job left her little time to socialize. But she occasionally dated the Oxford men who asked her to dinner and the theater on Saturday evenings. She enjoyed the social events and intellectual dialogue, but sometimes during the evening meals or theater, her mind split off and traveled thousands of miles back to Jerusalem and her conversations with Moshe.

She thought, *There's something about him. I could talk all night with him. We agreed to wait until we finished school to think about anything serious, but I wonder what he is doing tonight?* She decided to send him a letter. She pulled out her best stationery and started writing any thoughts that came to her mind, including thoughts about teaching, politics, her studies, family, and finances. She wrote many questions to Moshe about his life, thoughts, and beliefs. It was two in the morning when she put the twelve-page letter in the mailbox, kissing it before she dropped it in. *Here it goes! And here I come to you, Moshe!* she thought with a smile.

Finally, the long-awaited day came when Moshe's letter arrived. Fatima gleefully grabbed it and ran to her room. Breathlessly, she opened it and read through the five pages that he'd written in small, careful handwriting. She laughed and then she cried. After she finished reading the letter, she pulled out her stationery and started writing a response. Seven pages later, she signed her name and then ran to the mailbox, kissing the letter and dropping it in the mail slot.

This time Moshe responded to her with a phone call. It came in the evening when she was studying in her room. Her roommate knocked on her door and coyly said, "There is a man on the phone for you!" Fatima thought, *Who could that be?* After she said hello into the phone and heard the same one-word reply in Arabic, she knew it was Moshe. Her knees got so weak that she had to lean back on the wall to support herself.

Moshe and Fatima talked for an hour, until she realized how expensive it must be. "I'm so sorry! I must stop talking!" she said apologetically.

"Fatima, I could listen to you all night!" he said softly.

"Are you trying to make me fall for you?" she said with a laugh.

"It's always good for things to be mutual," he said suggestively.

She registered the meaning of his comment. She replied sweetly, "Moshe, it already is!"

Moshe and Fatima talked long-distance every Friday evening. When Moshe hurriedly excused himself after the Sabbath dinner, his parents thought that he was seeing a woman. They looked at each other and smiled secretively. But Moshe drove back to his apartment and called Fatima. She was always waiting by the phone, in order to ensure that her roommates would not talk to their boyfriends at the time of the prearranged Friday night talk.

At the end of the fall semester, Moshe asked Fatima how soon she was returning to Jerusalem. "I'll have a little time off in December. But I don't have enough money to visit my family—and you, if you want me to!" she explained with a little hesitation.

"Then I will visit you!" he replied warmly.

Her roommates agreed that Moshe could sleep on the couch for the week. "If he lasts that long on the couch!" they joked, winking suggestively.

Moshe arrived wreathed in smiles, bringing gifts for Fatima. They greeted each other as if they were long-lost friends separated for decades. They talked non-stop and laughed for hours. Fatima's roommates shared dinner with Moshe and Fatima. Her roommates whispered to each other when Moshe and Fatima were in the kitchen making water for tea, "Yes, indeed! They're in love!"

As predicted, Moshe did not last long on the couch. He joined Fatima's bed on the second night of his visit. She called out sick from work the next day. When they stumbled out for coffee in the morning, they discovered that Fatima's roommates had left for their jobs earlier than usual, leaving a note that read, *Enjoy the day! We won't be back until after 9 p.m.* Fatima and Moshe laughed and then looked at each other with alarm. "Did they hear us?" Fatima said.

Later, as they strolled hand in hand down Brick Lane to get Indian food for dinner, Moshe and Fatima started talking about the future.

"I know that nobody can predict the future, but I know that I want you in my future, Fatima." Moshe said softly.

"What? What are you saying?" Fatima said, stopping in the middle of the sidewalk.

"Yes, Fatima, I want to marry you. Will you?" Moshe hesitated.

Fatima looked at him and gently took his head between her heads. "I'm yours, fully and completely! But you have to ask me properly!" she said, kissing him playfully.

Sarah heard about Moshe and Fatima's wedding from one of her friends, who ran to her apartment with their wedding invitation. "He's marrying! He's marrying! Look!"

Sarah sat down on her couch and said, "Oh, what have I done? What have I thrown away? And he's marrying an Arab!" She started crying, and her friend tried to console her. "I tried to get him back," Sarah sobbed. "He was mine!"

She threw a vase across the room. It shattered against the wall, and she continued crying. *I shattered that temple! He won't break a glass at our wedding*, she thought as she cried on her friend's shoulder.

chapter 43

ITAMAR WAS AN ORTHODOX Jewish man who grew up in Safed, a village full of Jewish mystics. He had red hair, a red beard, Orthodox-type curly sideburns, and bright, sparkling blue eyes. He loved the mystical city that he grew up in but moved to Jerusalem the year before to be at the heart of Judaism. He was energized by the long debates in the synagogue on the Sabbath and studying the Torah all day with his friends.

After Itamar had finished his intense preparation for his bar mitzvah and celebrated the event with a big party at age thirteen, he started reading Western literature (without telling his parents). His friends lent him various books and magazines, sandwiching them between Israeli newspapers and passing them to him at school. He read a range of fiction and numerous American classics. Henry Miller was one of his favorites and brought him many ecstatic moments in the privacy of his bedroom. He spent hours in his cramped room reading under a small lamp. When the electricity went out, which it often did during the summer months when people used too many air conditioners, fans, and other devices to stay cool, he scrounged for a candle from the kitchen pantry and then lit it in his room. But that was dangerous because his mother could smell the candle and would find a feeble excuse to open his door to see what he was doing.

Itamar always had a copy of the Torah on his bed for the

moments when his mother rushed in. After calming his mother and promising to read only for one more hour, Itamar shut his door, dove back on his bed, and extracted a book by Miller from under his pillow. He devoured the writing, savoring Miller's free associations and adventures. Miller's flowing narrative shifted from scene to conversation to ideas to action so smoothly that Itamar would drink thirstily, as he would a glass of freshly squeezed orange juice. The books seduced him like he thought a woman would—they kept beckoning to him, taunting him, until he gave in and dove back into them. These writings were tasty to him compared to the dry, philosophical writing of the Torah. Itamar laid on his bed as if he were intoxicated, paralyzed by the new worlds opening up to him through written words and pictures.

For years, Itamar wanted a wife. He was twenty-four, well past the age he could marry. He was hungry for a woman. He told his parents that he wanted a wife, and they were ecstatic. To them, that meant that soon grandchildren would be on the way and that the house would again be busy and noisy. His mother immediately implemented her match-making skills. But it was difficult to find potential matches for Itamar because he was unemployed. Other mothers in the neighborhood had older sons who had dusty silver Hondas, their own fruit stalls at the market, or, better yet, an office position. Those mothers outmaneuvered her, to her great embarrassment.

Whenever Itamar walked down the dusty streets to visit his friends, he carefully looked over adolescent girls in long skirts and long-sleeved shirts, watching for any girl who looked him in the eye. Most would not. The occasional woman who locked eyes with him was someone who dwelled in the alley shadows. He knew that those women seduced men for money, a dangerous and immoral habit. But he had visited such women on the few occasions when he had money, such as when his uncles gave him money as birthday gifts.

Itamar knew that type of woman was "impure" and someone he could never marry. He wanted a fresh one when he married. He wanted to be the one to teach her the ways of love. And he wanted a woman no other man had touched or possessed. He wanted a woman who was holy, but not so holy that she did not want sex. He thought that her holiness would guarantee that she would not have sex with other men if she was bored with or angry at him, as in some of the scenes he read in the Henry Miller books. And her holiness would also make her devoted to him and willing to do whatever he asked. *If she claimed to serve God, then she also would serve me like a prince,* Itamar thought.

Like any young man, Itamar carefully watched the overtly sexual, young, secular Israeli women, and he desired them in his nightly dreams. But Itamar dreamed of having a shy, obedient Orthodox wife who would cook his meals, clean his clothes, maintain their spacious apartment, and have his babies, many of them. *She doesn't have to beautiful,* he thought. *In fact, it is better if she isn't, because if she is beautiful, then more men will desire her, whether she wears a headscarf or not. All I need is that she's fertile and can take care of our children. And cook a good meal!* he thought with smile. Itamar dreamed of one day moving to America and working for a computer company. He thought it would be an exciting life, to live there and have a great job, a loving woman, and a bunch of kids. *What else is there to life?* he thought.

In recent days, as Itamar stood in the synagogue and tried to focus on prayers with dozens of other men, his mind kept wandering to girls. He thought about girls he met at chaperoned events, girls he saw at stores but did not talk to, girls he saw going to school, and especially the girls he had neither seen in person nor talked to but who showed him the most private parts of their bodies in all sorts of poses in the magazines that his friends loaned him. It was the latter group that he visited every evening, "just to have a look." He revisited their memories all day long, whether or not he wanted to think about them.

Images of barely clothed bodies popped into his mind and transposed themselves over whatever he was thinking or doing. He was talking with a rabbi at the synagogue when the images from the previous evening slammed into his mental space and lingered. He suddenly became embarrassed, as if the images were also projected onto a screen that the rabbi could see. He quickly excused himself and ran to the dilapidated bathroom that had non-stop running water in the toilet and a leaky faucet. There, Itamar relieved himself of the sexual pressure, returning to the synagogue only after stopping by his friend's café for a smoke and a coffee. The rabbi never said anything to Itamar, yet he smiled knowingly when Itamar returned. That only added to Itamar's feelings of guilt.

Itamar had many friends who were Orthodox Jews and a whole different set of friends who were secular Jews. He preferred each group for different reason. The former group was better for intellectual discussions about the Torah and the latter group for fun. Itamar's group of secular friends knew how to joke, rebel, swear, and do whatever they felt like doing, as long as it was away from the eyes of older adults and parents. Itamar thought that his Orthodox friends were a little too serious about life. They were capable of triggering his feelings of guilt on practically any subject. His Orthodox friends always seemed to know what was proper to do at any moment, such as saying this or that prayer. While Itamar liked being part of the Orthodox community and understood its rules, he also thought that life was not as clear-cut as some of his younger Orthodox friends believed. He viewed their opinions as automatic responses to events that often needed to be considered, discussed, or analyzed to discern what should be done by whom and for what purpose.

While his secular friends seemed more free-spirited and spontaneous, Itamar noticed that people in the Orthodox community seemed to live with less anxiety and more joy and quiet confidence than his secular friends and their families. But he saw the flip side of orthodoxy, in that many were quick to ostracize others when they did not behave the expected way. *But maybe that is what it means to live by the rules. You notice who's not following the rules and try to do something about it,* he thought.

As he returned from the synagogue, Itamar thought, *I'm a believer, and I don't want to give that up. But guilt is a ready companion when you hang around a bunch of people who know exactly what to do and when. Sometimes I watch them angrily as they practice their ministrations and professions of faith so sincerely. They have no idea what goes on in my mind. I have so many impure thoughts, especially about sex, all the time.*

On a whim, Itamar decided to go buy a coffee at a coffee house. It was early afternoon, and he felt an urge to flee his parents' small apartment. He usually made his coffee at home to save money, but today was different. He walked into a coffee house and scanned the room to see if he knew anyone. His eyes fell on a young lady with long blond hair who was wearing a short dress and high heels and who was about to pay for a coffee. His mouth started watering. *Yum!* he thought. He smiled as he walked up behind her. He looked at her face and impulsively said, "Can I pay for your coffee?"

She turned around to look at him. "It depends," she said.

"On what?" Itamar said with a smile. He already liked her.

"On what you want from me," she said, smiling back at him.

"That all depends on you, doesn't it?" he quipped.

"Good response! Not the typical 'Whatever you've got to offer' response!" she said, and they both laughed.

"Please, permit me the honor of buying you a coffee and

conversing with you for a moment," Itamar said in his most gracious voice, bowing slightly, his hand on his heart.

"Ah, a gentleman is among us!" she said with a big smile. "My name is Sarah."

"Itamar, at your service." He gestured for her to find a seat.

After paying for the coffee and carrying it to the table that Sarah had picked, Itamar started talking with Sarah, and they did not stop until the coffee shop closed at 9:00 p.m. that night. He invited her to dinner at a modest but tasty restaurant the next evening, and she accepted. They exchanged phone numbers as they left the coffee shop.

"May I walk you home?" Itamar asked, opening the door for Sarah and watching her walk out.

"Thank you, but I have to take a bus home from here," she said.

"No, let me pay for a taxi for you," he insisted. She tried to refuse, but he was already hailing a taxi. He opened the door for her and then asked for the address. He gave the driver sufficient money and then bid Sarah goodnight.

She rolled down the window and yelled, "Thank you, Itamar!"

He yelled a good-bye back to her and then thought, *How am I going to pay for all this?*

chapter 44

ON THE INTERNATIONAL RETURN flight back home, Rachel thought sadly, *I don't know if it was worse living with a man who never touched me anymore or to live alone like I do now. When I was young, I had a romanticized view of marriage—the loving forever mantra with a fluffy white dress and sweet wedding, after which I'd give myself fully and passionately to a man. Those stereotypes of a good man-woman relationship, like picnics in the park and long walks on the beach, were supposed to mean that you were communicating nicely with each other. In a perfect world, there is never anger, arguments, jealousy, control, manipulation, duplicity, or hiding one's own real thoughts.*

I want a peaceful relationship, not one that I always doubt, not always wondering what he meant, what he is doing, and whether he loves me. Sex can often be brief, leaving twenty-three and a half hours a day in which the couple has to get along, make decisions together, and have fun together in the community, Rachel mused.

With those thoughts, Mr. Hit-and-Run appeared in her mind. She remembered that he'd walked her back to her hotel room when they were at a conference. She asked him if he wanted to come in. He said, "Thanks, another time," and ran off. *Maybe that meant he is a moral man?* she thought. *Or maybe it meant he's too busy to have an affair? Maybe he's gay? Or maybe he is having an affair with someone else? Or maybe he prefers to play with himself rather than giving love to another person?* She chuckled and then frowned at the tsunami of thoughts that hit her.

But I don't want an affair. I don't know what's really going on with Mr. Hit-and-Run. He's seriously nervous whenever he is near me, but he says nothing to me about his feelings. I remember meeting his wife and seeing how they interacted. They were tense and irritable with each other. If a relationship has run its course, then why do they pretend otherwise? His wife seems like an aggressive woman. Maybe he's puzzled about her but then forgets it all when she serves him his dinner! Rachel thought with a smirk. *I need to stop thinking about him and move on. Maybe I should post a personal classified ad.* She got out her pen and small notebook and wrote:

> *Looking for a man who is intellectually curious, open-minded, hard-working, moral, and trustworthy. Seeking a man with positive communication and emotional connection skills with a woman other than his mother. Seeking a man who has sex only in the context of love and who prefers the real thing more than a video. Must have a full-time job, shave, understand what a laundry basket signifies, chew with his mouth closed, and know how to use a Kleenex. Knowing how to read and write is a must. If you aren't scared of being real with me, send me a message!*

Rachel put her notebook away and chuckled at her impulsive writing. She thought about how she'd once told her friends, "I am acquired taste for men. They may not fall in love with me immediately, but if they stick around and get past my defenses, they find a sweet, pleasing lover."

She started musing again. *I bet most men have no idea how sexually wild I can be with a guy when I'm in love. And I don't use sex to extract what I want from a man. I think that's cruel. I want to feel a man's love before I exchange sexual intimacies with a man again. I know that I'm quite capable of deep love and sex. But my love is intricately and beautifully interwoven with my sexual energy, like a tapestry. And someday I will take a man on a fantastic carpet ride!* She smiled to herself.

Rachel stared out the airplane window into the dark sky and thought about her unruly imagination and frustrated longing for him. She remembered sitting at a conference banquet a few feet away from Mr. Hit-and-Run. She thought, *During the banquet, I kept imagining that if I were his wife, I'd be hanging all over him, holding on to his arm, kissing his cheek, ruffling his hair, and flirting with him all the time. I felt a raging desire to take him into a dark room and rip his clothes off. But we just sat there listening to speakers and daintily eating our food. If he only knew how, in one single moment, he could have had me on my knees, melting before him, melting into him, melting with him. If he just touched me and held me briefly, I would've fallen. Damn, if I was a different kind of woman, I would've loved him and rocked his world that night!*

I am getting fed up with my own fantasies, Rachel thought. *I don't want to have an affair. The Ten Commandments warn against adultery, and I know about the many psychological dynamics that make love triangles very unstable. But there is no commandment against divorce. The bottom line is if he really wanted to be with me, he'd do something about it and make a change for me. And he has not.*

I also don't want to change. I have been stuck hoping that he'd change and become mine. That is just a delusion! she scolded herself. *No need to analyze anything—just stop this repetitive, boring, predictable, inane, stupid, stultifying thinking! It's like spinning my wheels a million times! I need a new mantra.* As tears welled in her eyes, she wrote this poem:

> So many thoughts unspoken
> So many words unsaid.
> Life as I wished it
> Will change in the days ahead.
>
> My will is not broken
> Although my heart may be
> Change you will never,
> Nor I an accomplice be.
>
> Crooked truths of my own creation
> Led me down this path
> But time to venture onward
> Without regrets about the past:
> Time to stop looking back.

After writing, she sat stunned and quiet. *Something has changed irrevocably, somewhere along the road, somewhere deep in my soul. I've loved him deeply, but what can you do if someone does not want to love you back?* She sighed deeply, closed her eyes, and tucked the airplane blanket around her body.

Rachel arrived at her New York City apartment, unlocked the door, and wearily dragged her suitcases into the foyer. She wiggled her feet into her fluffy pink slippers. *It's his loss. I'm sure that he doesn't understand the power of my love and all of its ramifications and what he's missing out on. I know I am middle-age, but so will be the next man I date. Maybe another guy will be more grateful and appreciative of what I could give to him!* She ran down the hall to her freezer, where her favorite soother was hiding—coffee ice cream with chocolate flakes. After a few minutes of gustatory orgasms from her favorite ice cream, Rachel put on her running shoes and dashed out the door. *Fresh air and exercise! That's what I need to release my worries and to be free.*

She ran down two streets and approached a man watering a vegetable garden in his two-by-two-foot plot in front of his townhouse. He looked Zen-like, with his dreamy expression and calm demeanor. Rachel squeaked out a hello as she approached him. He looked startled, but he turned his head and mumbled a greeting. His eyes scanned her body as she ran. She turned her head back just as he was dropping his eyes to her lovely, firm bottom. She smiled. *It'd be nice, someday ...* Adrenaline and the coffee ice cream kicked in, and she rapidly jogged, as if none of her muscles hurt.

She returned to her apartment and stood in the middle of her living room, picturing Mr. Hit-and-Run. *In my heart of hearts, I believe that there is nobody like you, and there never will be. But no more fantasy loves! I need reality. I need someone who will hold me and love me, a man who goes for what he wants. I'd marry you in an instant if you asked me. I know that you do not want that. I will look for another man--but I still love you!* she thought sadly. Then she yelled out loud, "But I am done with you, man! So done with you!" She briskly pulled the shades closed, sat down at her desk, grabbed a piece of paper and purple pen, and quickly wrote:

You rocked
my world
but why
didn't
you
make me
sing?

She stared at the words she had just written. "Good-bye, my love. I've loved you dearly. But it is time to move on," she whispered to herself. She turned out the light.

chapter 45

ITAMAR AND SARAH MET again the very next evening at a café on Sderot Golda Meir and again talked for hours. They talked about their lives, their schooling, their families, their beliefs, and their hopes for the future. Nothing was out of bounds.

"I have to tell you something," Sarah said, looking at Itamar seriously.

"Sure! Is something wrong? Did I say something that upset you?" he said with a frown.

"No. Not at all. It's just that I think you need to know that my mother is not Jewish. I grew up in a household that practiced both Jewish and Christian rituals to reflect my parents' heritage. I got the best of both worlds. Or at least, a lot of celebrations!" They laughed together. "But you know, for years, I've been reading about Judaism. And in some ways, I find it more appealing than Christianity."

For the first time that evening, Itamar looked shocked. "What? Why would that be?"

Sarah smiled when she saw his confused expression and started telling him what she perceived as the differences between Christian religious practices, especially the American forms, and Jewish religious practices. "I've also found it really interesting to observe the differences between Orthodox and secular women in Israel."

"Please, tell me more!" Itamar implored.

"Well, it seems to me that secular Israeli women are tough about romance and aggressive about bedding men. Maybe it's because the women serve two years in the military and that heightens their awareness of life and death. I know the secular girls view Orthodox girls as idealistic, impractical, and rigid prudes. I have even heard the secular girls snidely call the Orthodox girls the "Chosen of the Chosen." And it seems like Orthodox girls view the secular ones as wild, cynical, immoral, seductive, and caustic beings, who may be Jewish in name but are impure, a stain on Jewish lineage."

"And what else have you observed?" he said with a smile.

"Some of the Orthodox girls explained to me that they fall in love as rapidly as the secular girls, but they never verbalize it because it's not permissible. And they told me that many of them write their romantic wishes in their secret, locked diaries or write their beloved's name on a piece of paper and discretely place it in a crack in the Western Wall in Jerusalem. Or they write his name on one side of a rock and bury it in a secret spot in the field, or they scratch the boy's name on the underside of the drawer of their desk at home or on the backside of their closet."

Itamar chuckled at Sarah's statement and said, "What else have you observed, Madame Therapist?"

"Well, it seems that for many people, Israeli life promotes quick sexual decisions. Life is to be lived as fast as possible, because tomorrow is unknown and uncertain. Many girls think, *Who knows whether I'll be at the wrong place at the wrong time next week when a terrorist decides to trigger a suicide bomb? So I must experience life now, and not wait!* And because the men they date often aren't ready to consider marriage, the men run away at the first sign of marriage pressure. So the women's cynicism grows out of repeated hurt and disappointment. Their sexual coupling only lasts a brief while, with little emotional connection, which makes the women feel like prostitutes."

"Ah, now you are getting to the heart of the matter!" Itamar exclaimed, and they both laughed.

"Seems like this is problematic because men no longer seek a woman as a life partner, only as a night partner. I know that many call women who wait until marriage for sex naive, but I now think that those who have sex on the first or second date are even more naive. They are blind to the reality of humanity, to the nasty and mean side of people and the possibility that they could be physically hurt by their sex partner. And they deny that building trust is important for a healthy relationship. More and more I think that moral rules help to eliminate the gray zones in life and help us have healthier relationships," Sarah said.

"Good to hear you say that! Orthodox Judaism has many rules, and I am proud that I am an Orthodox Jew!" Itamar exclaimed. "And you know, a lot of debating goes on in Orthodox circles. Our understanding is constantly evolving, and I think that is something secular people miss, especially when they look at our clothes." They both laughed.

Sarah replied, "As I grow older, I realized how important moral rules are. Morality is boring for many people, especially for the young and frisky, who think that they know best and that rules are too constricting. Some even run around acting like Nietzsche's supermen, above the law. But I think when you try to live with someone, that's when you realize how important morality is. I think the less moral your partner is, the more you try to control them and the less you trust them."

"Wow, I like your impressive insight into human nature!" Itamar said to Sarah.

"Thanks, but often the light comes after darkness," she said, a bit sadly.

"That's okay. At least you are there now." Itamar replied and looked at her intently, his blue eyes sparkling.

"Well, now I know how I want to live!" Sarah said. "Marriage is a collision and fusion of two worlds, a nexus between the body and spirit, the ideal and the real, the private and the shared, the individual and the couple. So there should be rules that help govern that collision," she said with a smile.

"Could you ever become an Orthodox Jew?" Itamar asked, returning her smile.

"Yes, because it's been making more and more sense to me. I've read a lot of Jewish writings, including books on Jewish views on sexuality," she replied with an impish grin. "But seriously, I think both Judaism and Christianity express the desire to seek God, to move toward God, to attempt communication with God, and to find meaning and order in a chaotic world. After all, Abraham, the first Jew, became a man of faith by listening to and trusting God."

Itamar nodded in agreement.

Sarah continued, "You know, I started thinking recently that our culture of women wanting to seduce and be seduced actually promotes women's disrespect for themselves and a dissociation of sexuality from any higher meaning. It's like tasting the knowledge from the tree of Good and Evil in the Garden of Eden. We were warned not to, but we jumped in. And we forgot that there was another tree in the Garden of Eden—the tree of life. And to me, that means that there is a better, healthier way!"

"The more you talk, the more appealing an Eve you become!" Itamar joked.

"And I never met an Adam who understands me until I met you!" Sarah said smiling and blushing.

Sarah watched Itamar walk back from the restroom. *He talks with such sincerity and honesty! He is really different from any man I've ever met. I think I can really trust him!* she thought with a smile.

What a babe! She is so smart and easy to talk to! And she wants everything that I want! And I think she likes me! Itamar thought, grinning broadly as he sat down beside Sarah.

After they finished dinner, they took a walk through the Old City of Jerusalem. As they exited the Old City, he bought her an ice cream, and they sat outside the walls of the Old City and looked at the panorama before them. He gently grabbed her hand, pulled her close, and kissed her. She responded to his kiss.

Then he whispered, "You're the one for me! Will you marry me?"

Startled, she pulled back from him, hesitated for a moment, and then whispered with a huge smile, "Yes, but give me time to get used to you."

Itamar said nothing, but he nodded to Sarah. He sat back and grinned expansively, thinking, *Blessed be God! You are almighty, the king of my soul! Thank you, most holy God, for sending her to me!*

chapter 46

KING SOLOMON SOLEMNLY STROLLED down the dirt lane, past the small stone houses where women used to sweep, cook, and wash laundry with their children running around in circles, laughing and yelling with shrieks of joy. He remembered how the women used to bow their heads as he walked by. Their children used to stop their games momentarily and watch Solomon walk past in his expensive clothes, with his gold-handled sword and wide gold belt. But today, because of the fighting outside of the city gates, they all were hiding in their homes out of fear.

Solomon knew that his kingdom was in danger of falling. His advisors had just told him that his troops were losing in battle at this very moment. He could hear the clink of metal, the screams of fallen men, and the low rumble of the battle.

God, where are you? he thought as he walked through the abandoned marketplace.

Solomon went back to his chambers, where an Egyptian wife had set up altars to Molech and Ashtoret. "For your protection," she had whispered when she showed him the altars.

He bowed in front of the altars and said a prayer for intervention. "Help me, gods! Where are you? I will do whatever you want if you save my kingdom."

Solomon thought about all the years he had spent chasing works of beauty—whether the artistic details that beautified the holy temple, the fragrant charms of a lovely woman, or the celebration of culture throughout his land. Now he wished that he was more like his father, King David, the warrior king. He looked at his flabby arms and bountiful stomach, which was like the stomach of a well-fed baby.

Why did I not train my men better for this? Why did I chase Truth and Beauty instead? he thought. He sat down at the table where he had read thousands of scrolls and written countless words documenting his thoughts and efforts at justice. He looked at what he wrote recently, "He who rules his spirit is better than he who takes a city" and thought, *But now they are going to take my city.* He rolled up the document, placed it in a special storing jar, stood up briskly, and growled, "They may defeat me, but they will never break me."

He walked back to the altars and stretched out before them. He fell asleep in front of the silent statues until nightfall.

Solomon's advisors ran into his chambers and woke him up. They told him that Hadad's troops were slaughtering his men on the battlefield. He gave them the command to call for a retreat, to pull back into the city walls. His advisors ran out to give the orders.

Solomon looked out in the direction of the battlefield and thought, *This soon will be over. My kingdom is falling, and it is out of my control!* He walked over to the altars to Molech and Ashtoret and pummeled them with a stick. "You lie to me! You can't help me! You won't protect us!" He smashed the clay figures on the altars and the bowls that held the food sacrifices. "You are not God!" He pushed the altars over and stomped on them.

Then Solomon fell on his knees and buried his face in his hand. He moaned softly and said, "What have I done?" He fell to the ground and stretched out, prostrate. "God of Abraham, Isaac, and Jacob, hear me now! I understand now that You are

God of All Gods. Forgive me! I have done wrong! Save us! Save your people!" he yelled again and again as tears filled his eyes.

Solomon fasted for hours, taking neither food nor water from his servant. Every hour or two, his advisors ran into his room to update him. Solomon gave orders to his advisors, and they ran out without taking food or water. He paced like a lion around his rooms throughout the night. He anxiously listened for a response from the God of Abraham, Isaac, and Jacob. There was none. He kept falling to his knees, moaning deeply, tears pouring freely, whispering entreaties to the God he had abandoned.

In the predawn hours, when the birds started warbling their morning songs to the sun, Solomon stood up and grabbed a blank scroll. He quickly wrote:

> In my frightened freedom
> I ran blindly
> Not knowing that
> You loved
> My fragile being
> And waited for me
> Silently.
>
> Forgive me
> Oh God of Abraham!
> I have done wrong.
> Save your people!
> But I know that
> In the end
> Your Will be done.

He walked out into the courtyard and looked out beyond the walls of Jerusalem. He saw the glint of armor from thousands of men. There was roaring, growling, and screaming. He whispered to himself, "My glorious kingdom will fall. What have I done?"

He washed his hands, splashed his face, and drank from the stream of water that spewed from a gilded lion's mouth in the courtyard. He thought, *This may be my last drink of water.* He called for his armor, which was placed on him with speedy care. He marched out of his palace and faced his men, who had retreated behind the city walls. "Let us fight in honor, until the end!" he roared, holding up his sword. "Let us protect our temple!" he bellowed. In response, his men cheered while thrusting their swords in the air. Solomon turned toward the horizon and saw it lined with a river of glinting swords and spears.

About the Author

Zoe Senesh is the pen name for a woman who loves to travel in the Middle East and other areas of the world. She has an advanced degree in social sciences and lives in the northwestern United States.

Printed in the United States
By Bookmasters